NO LACK OF LONESOME

by

Albino Gonzales

ISBN -0-9679855-2-4
Library of Congress Catalog Card No. 2001 131430

Cover art by Ximena Gonzales
Copyright © 2001 by Ximena Gonzales

Farolito Press
P.O. Box 60003
Grand Junction, CO 81506

Manufactured in the United States of America
Pyramid Printing and Copy Center
Grand Junction, Colorado
www.pyramidprinting.com

For
Ismo
who loves trucks
Chalina
who loves to read
&
Ise
Arias
Marina
Ariela
Ximena
all
Míos y Mías

Para

You are an inspiring educator who has touched many lives. God bless you for the impact you had on my Sons - Arias.

H-10-01

Forward

A novel is not a poem, but if there ever
could be a novel that is poetry, this is it.

L. Luis López
Musings of a Barrio Sack Boy
A Painting of Sand

About the Author

Albino Gonzales was born in Guadalupita, New Mexico. His childhood in that rural setting included members of his extended family which included grandparents and great grandparents with whom he experienced strong ties through the traditional folklore, the cuentos and adivinanzas. The Spanish folklore of Northern New Mexico inspires Gonzales' work.

Gonzales holds a doctorate from Arizona State University. His dissertation, which explores the theory of linguistic relativity, examines literature written bilingually and its potential in promoting multilingual literacy. Winner of the 1996 Translation of Poetry Award by the World Congress of Poets through International Laureates for Children, by the Chiu Shui Poetry Quarterly, Taiwan, Republic of China, Gonzales is President-CEO of Juventud Multilingual Press, Grand Junction, Colorado. He is also a professor at Mesa State College in Grand Junction, Colorado.

Suddenly I

I round the corner, glance to my right, and there, reflected in the window along with the rest of Mary Constable's Thrifts and Curios, am I.

In the pane of the thrift shop, the street crowds around me make their way among and through the dusty second-hands inside. A red-black booklet under a mound of empty canning jars catches my eye. I step into the half-light of the shop, and, through the umber, find my way to the shelf. Removing the writing tablet carefully from beneath the hill of glass, I dust the bonnet feathers of the Indian sketched on the tablet's cover.

The ink lines around the plumes are weak.

I blow on the face, but time has worked dust well into the eyes.

Picking up the Big Chief tablet, I tilt it toward the window for a closer look.

Light passing through the warped and aged glass strikes the cover and appears to stir the plumes.

Curious to find in the abandoned tablet childhood meanderings in crayon streaks, I take Big Chief to the window and leaf through his pages.

All are flat and empty.

Flipping the tablet shut, I place it on the sill. A moment later I retrieve it to return it to its place under the jars.

I run my hand across the cover.

Big Chief's face is warm.

Our eyes meet.

He stares at me.

Sitting on the window ledge, I place him on my lap.

Warpage of glass and sun weave mystery in the bower of light that fills the thrift window. On my lap the Indian trembles upward through the dust, grateful, as if remembering sun after years of amber under the hill of empty jars.

In the warped light of the shop we stare at each other until the eyes water, remembering...

... the top of the hill.

Folding back the feather bonnet on Big Chief's head to the first blank page, I reach for a pen.

Carly in the Window

A.C.'s mother brought the shiny new car to a gentle stop, and he opened the front door.

"Hello," she greeted, as I climbed over his arithmetic tablet and sat between her and A.C. Everything, from the leather-lined seats that matched the door panels up to the velvet roof, smelled like the inside of a new purse.

With her small hand barely on the wheel, she leaned lightly to the left and the car responded. We were on our way to school. I had never been in an airplane before, but I was sure this was what it was. As we floated along, the sky stood still while the tree tops glided by. When the sun glared too hot through the window, she cooled it down with a rush of air by playing her fingers lightly on three silver buttons beside the wheel.

Feeling the magical breeze, I leaned back to enjoy the fantasy machine. With every movement she made sailing the plane, she repeated herself gracefully three times in the shiny marbles. In the window beside her, she appeared like a beautiful glass doll. Leaning forward for a better look at her, I drew close to the three steelies where her fingers had played, but as I approached them, she disappeared and I was in the knobs, potato-nosed and frog-eyed ugly. With a quick jerk I leaned back against the seat and watched A.C.'s mother return to the roundy curves.

I studied her, both in the silver balls and where she sat beside me. Her eyelashes were curvy long. And the freckles on her nose, perfect, in the right spot, not too many. She looked down at me, smiled, then, glancing ahead, moved the wheel slightly to her left. The airplane swayed gently as it followed after the curve of her hand, and my heart went right behind it.

A.C's mom was beautifulest right beneath the curls where her ears ended and the long earrings began. The dangly beebees looked like babies climbing all over each other, each wanting to be first to whisper in her ear. Every morning she wore a new pair. Today they were silver; yesterday they were gold.

I wondered what her name was. If it was Caroline, I would probably call her Carly. The freckles on her nose made her look like a Carly. Secretly, I wished Nana could be like her. If I had a mother like Carly, I thought, the first thing I'd do would be to have her bring party cookies to school at least once a week. Then I'd have her teach every Friday like A.C.'s mother did. She always made the answers easier.

I looked at A.C.

He's smart because his mother is so beautiful, I thought. I looked away from him and back at Carly in time to see her place her foot on a pedal. Her hands were perfect, but her feet were perfecter. With only one little tap on the pedal, she steered the airplane gently around a gust of wind and back straight. She was shiny clean everywhere, her clothes, the glass on her glasses, even her princess fingernails.

She looked down at me and winked.

For a moment, my heart flew ahead of the airplane.

Her teeth were the perfectest I had ever seen.

I stretched my hand in her direction to touch the closest knob, but when I touched the silver, it was cold from the magical air.

She took her foot off one pedal, barely placed it on another, and pressed down lightly. The plane came to a gentle landing. I sat up and looked out. We were in front of the schoolhouse.

"Good-by," she said, pulling the door shut after I had followed A.C. out of the car.

I reached the doorway and turned around for one last look. The car was vanishing around a curve, but in my mind I could still see Carly in the window.

Carly followed me to every class. In arithmetic, I finished the twenty-five addition problems as fast as I could. I guessed on many of the subtractions, finished before anyone else, and started to draw on the side. Of the nine pairs of hands I drew, none looked like Carly's. The fingers were either too thick or too thin and none of the nails matched Carly's.

On my health assignment, I didn't know half the words so I skipped over them. I was first to finish the lung lesson and spent the rest of the period looking at the beautiful princess in my mind.

In art, as we worked on the earrings we were making for our mothers, I pretended I was making my jewelry for Carly, not for Nana. I was very careful with them, rubbing them extra shiny on the edges making sure the curves of one earring matched those of the other. I measured every string three times to make sure all of them were exactly the same length and that they looped just right. Even though the earrings were only salt crystals made from colored water and flour paste tied to fishing twine, they sparkled like real gems on the wet thread. Tomorrow morning, I thought, as I eyed the glinting salt, I might even ask A.C. what her name was.

That afternoon when Carly and A.C. dropped me off after school, I watched them sail away in the magical machine. The long, low car slipped away obeying every curve of Carly's beautiful hand until it disappeared. I knew neither of them was looking back, but I still waved. It was a happysad goodbye. Half of me was happy because I had made the earrings for Carly, the other half was sad because I still had her treasure in my hand.

The sad side won out.

I knew we would never have a car like that. Nana said as long as we lived on their way to school and as long as they were willing to pick me up, there would be no need for one. And we would never live anywhere else, either.

Our little farm was where she had grown up. "We have all we need here," she was always saying, "the garden, the fruit trees, the well beside the small stream." She never forgot to mention her goats, and of course, she always had to throw in her ten million chickens. That's what I hated most, the stupid chickens. Especially in spring when they went around half feathered with their legs bony pink and scaly all over. Of all the animals on the farm, the chickens were the ones that took the longest to feed. All she ever killed were the old ones that were tough to eat. For any other supplies we might need, she would simply tell me to give A.C.'s mother the message and she would purchase them in town for us. On her way back, she left them in a box under the bench beside the tall cottonwood at the entrance to our pathway. From there I would carry them home.

Chickens, goats, fruit trees, and a garden with a well beside the stream, I thought again.

I sighed.

The lastest thing on earth I would ever want to be was a farmer.

5

Salt and Grasshoppers

I walked up our stone path slowly. I looked down at the earrings in my hands. As I thought about how they would have looked against Carly's beautiful skin, they felt like a stolen treasure. It would be best to throw them away. I put my tongue to the sharp edges of the crystals. The salt spread crabapple sour through my mouth.

Still some distance from the house, I could see Nana moving about in a small cloud of dust as she prepared her garden. That meant there were only a few weeks left of school. This time of year especially, she was always digging somewhere when I came home. Her faded clothes looked like her flower garden in August when the rains failed. August and September both were too hot for even a short walk, and everything looked old and wilted.

She seemed deep in thought as she slammed her hoe into the earth. At times she dug away at the same spot over and over even after she had already mowed down the weed.

She stopped hoeing, and said something. She was probably talking to one of her chickens. She spoke louder, almost at a shout and then hit the ground extra hard. She was probably after Top Feathers, the ragged hen who led the whole flock of trouble everywhere. That old feather bag with the scaliest legs was probably scratching in the garden where she was not supposed to.

Nana's back was curved toward me as she hoed. She wore her long, brown sweater. As she attacked the weeds, she moved her head slightly up and down in rhythm with the hoe and her hair followed, but even with the sun on it, her's was not half as shiny as Carly's curls.

She was wearing her favorite apron with the heavy denim straps and enormous matching pockets. The faded pink print was the newest of the four she owned. If she had at least twice as many aprons, I thought, she would look prettier. Denim on flannel, I thought with some embarrassment as I continued watching her dig up dust, what dumb cloth.

6

If only she looked like Carly, my grades probably would be better. I wouldn't have to worry about passing, either. There was no doubt in my mind I would be called on to lead the class more often whenever we went anywhere. And her name! I wished I could change it to Nan.

Stopping at the grocery bench under the oak, I stacked my books on one end and sat on them. What would it be like if A.C. and I were brothers? We would have our own rooms. We could probably share a lot of our clothes back and forth. Dinner would be great and afterward, we'd talk.

Carly's beautiful hand around a glass filled with cold juice came into my mind. She set it before me without a ripple on the red and as smoothly as she had landed the plane in front of the schoolhouse. In her other hand, she was holding two plates. She placed mine on the table first, and then A.C.'s. It was quail, not old chicken, and beside the wonderful meat, not fruit dried to chip, but the real thing, a fresh apple.

"Rough day at school?" she asked. "You look a little sad. School's about out if that's what's troubling you."

Nana's voice jarred me. I had been so busy watching Carly serve my brother and me breakfast I hadn't noticed her come down the path to sit beside me. She reached for my hand. It wasn't smooth like Carly's, perfect on the wheel, but rough like the wooden handle of the hoe. Under her nails were bits of dirt.

I pulled away.

How could I tell her what was bothering me? Not only did she not look like Carly, what did she know about school? What lesson would she ever be able to teach? I looked at her two missing teeth. What would the class think about that if she ever came to help out like Carly?

I cracked open my fist and looked at the earrings hidden in my hand, then up at her ear and pictured them there. No. They did not belong there. Besides, her hair was too long. Nana didn't have enough curl.

"Come on," she said. "It's good to talk and for people to walk together. Give me your hand. What say we go for a little walk?"

I remained quiet for a moment.

"Want to?" she persisted, squeezing my hand again. I felt the salt dig into my palm.

"Where are we going?" I asked flatly, pulling my hand away and looking as far away into space as I could.

"Oh, everywhere and nowhere. To the top of the hill," she said, winking as though she were keeping a secret. She always winked when she was hiding something she wanted to surprise me with. It was her way of telling me that whatever she was hiding could jump out at any moment and that I should be on the lookout.

"Everywhere and nowhere," she repeated. She laughed the half-laugh that came before her surprises. I wondered what everyone would think about that too if she ever came to school. And there was that wink again! How I wished she would stop it. Again she laughed, and her eyes laughed with her.

She rose from the old bench and looked down on me like scaly-legged Top Feathers when she was teaching one of her stupid chicks how to pull a worm out of the ground.

"Are things not going well at school?"

"No, everything is fine," I said, as boringly as I could so she would stop her pecking. As I answered, the earring salt cut into my tongue, sour like green apples from the crab tree. In my hand, I could feel the jewels burning. She motioned me to stand up, but I played chick-stupid and pretended not to hear.

She was standing, I was sitting. I looked at her through the sun. There was silence. I didn't speak to her because I was far away, on the far edge of the bench.

She sat back down. "Maybe I should go to your class and..."

"No, no!" I interrupted quickly, reaching for a book and pulling it out from under me. "I have all my work here and everything is fine. I've done all my homework and everything is turned in. I even have two check pluses in health." As I spoke, the salt crabbing on my tongue didn't feel as sharp.

"When A.C.'s mother dropped off the supplies last month, she told me your teacher is planning a school day for parents in a couple of weeks. She said all the parents are invited and..."

"Well, not all the parents go," I interrupted, hoping to end any possibility of her showing up at school. "Those things aren't that important, you know."

Nana licked her lips and her eyes pinched up a little as if she had come across some sudden salt.

"Oh?" she answered, her voice trailing off in wounded surprise. Then, finding comfort in herself, she continued. "Well, if they don't all go, then I guess I won't go either." Though she acted satisfied with my explanation and her decision, she edged slightly away from me toward the far end of the bench.

"You don't have to worry. Everything is fine at school," I said, wishing to wash the wound in her voice.

"Are you sure?" she asked, pretending hope.

"Oh, yes. A.C.'s mom isn't going either." I noticed the sour crab had all but left my mouth. I breathed in deep and fresh and looked into her face hoping she had not noticed my relief, but she looked away. As she stared away, I slipped the earrings into my pocket.

She remained quiet for a few minutes tracing her finger around a sun-eaten rose on her apron. She outlined the first blossom, then jumped to another flower worn weak-pink by the sun. She traced several more roses in silence, then, grasping a handful of the apron flowers, she crumpled the rag as if drying her hands and dropped it back on her lap.

"I can see that if it doesn't rain soon," she said, without looking at me, "grasshoppers will be a problem this year. Already I can tell my favorite little rose is not doing well." I looked into her face, but she looked away.

She placed both hands on her lap. Then she spread her fingers wide and smoothed the roses she had wrinkled against her legs for several minutes without saying anything. After she ironed the weak blooms, she stared at her hands for a moment, rubbing one with the other slightly as if washing them with invisible water. She looked at them again, slipped them under her apron, but right away brought them back out. Placing them slowly on her lap, she turned them upward and faced her nails. Quietly, she began to dig them clean. She had barely cleaned the first nail when she stopped and pushed her sleeves up a little. She folded her hands on her lap, then, with long strokes, smoothed out a long scar on her arm. When she pressed her arm free of blood the scar disappeared, but once the veins flowed again, the long tissue stood out shiny against her brown skin.

"Does it hurt a lot?" I asked, anxious to know what she had been thinking, and feeling somewhat guilty.

She bit her lip and licked it. Her face was still tight.

"Oh, grasshoppers are always hard on people. Hard on everything. They are salt that dries up whatever is in its path. They go beyond the blood sometimes and suck out the heart from anything that moves."

She ironed another rose, then, without looking at me, she continued. "Ugly little thoughts is what they are, born out of nowhere, and this summer I fear will be the worst."

Satisfied that grasshoppers in her garden was the problem and not what I had said, I made sure she stayed on the scar.

"No, I mean the scar, what happened there?"

I reached for her arm, but she pulled it away and looked at it closely as though the old wound were a new surprise.

She remained silent for a few moments staring at the scar. Then, without looking up and as if she were talking to it she said, "I bet you think I was never young, don't you?"

She smoothed her face with both hands, but as soon as she let go, the wrinkles all came back.

"Skin gets too set in its ways sometimes. Starts when a person is very young. Too much being in the world under the sun. They say skin remembers."

Her voice sounded sad as it did when her vegetables ended up runty because there had been too many bugs. She started to speak, but didn't. She looked in the direction of her garden, but beyond it. I followed her eyes, but couldn't tell where she was looking.

"How did you get that scar?"

She looked again at the old wound and patted it gently. She rose from the grocery bench and tried to smile. "I'll tell you when we get to the top of the hill. We can't talk here. This place is jumping with grasshoppers."

She looked at me, away, then back at me again.

"Come on," she said, pulling me firmly away from the book stack and onto the gravel road. "Let's walk. And leave your books here."

The First Fruit

We walked alone. She was on the right track, I was on the left.

We went quietly past several neighbors who were preparing their plots for spring planting. Our closest one was returning from the hill behind his house with an armload of wood.

Nana waved and he, raising the extra stick he carried in one hand, greeted her.

"Looks like he's going to be busy," she said. "Cottonwood root's the best there is. It's softer."

I refused to answer.

We went by our next neighbor. He was in his orchard standing under a tall grapevine.

Nana waved, but he, pretending to be busy pruning, clipped away two inches from the branch without a wave.

"Well, doesn't surprise me," Nana said. "That's why he lives alone. Can't get along with anybody. Just like his father. Sad even kin can't get along."

"He grows the best apples, though," I challenged.

Nana ignored my remark and continued in silence.

"Sometimes it doesn't matter if you're a boy or a girl," she said, after we had gone past the orchard. She was not looking at me, but at the ground in front of her. Her hands were clasped together behind her back, making her curve downward a little more than usual. Her apron floated before her as if clearing a path.

"In many things people are all very much alike, you know. Many times there is no lack of lonesome. Even for grown-ups, too."

Lack of lonesome was her way of saying something was not going quite as it should.

"Want to talk?" she asked again, as she glanced up from the dirt track for the first time and looked directly at me. Her eyes searched my face as though knowing I was holding something back.

"There's nothing to talk about. It's just that..."

"People used to say," she interrupted, "there is no ailment that lasts a hundred years, neither a man who can bare it. I think it's true." Sometimes she used words I didn't understand. "What does that mean?"

"Ailment? Ailment is anything that's bothering us."

"Well, nothing's bothering me," I said almost harshly, looking back into my track. I put my hand in my pocket and rolled the sharp salt through my fingers. Though I walked with my eyes in the rut, I could feel her eyes heavy on me. I felt like one of Top Feather's idiot-chicks when the old hen stood over it pecking at it for an explanation as to why the worm had escaped down the hole. Her eyes continued on me. Knowing that Nana was a hen that pecked away until she pulled out the worm, I knew I had to say something to satisfy her.

"Oh, we just have to write poems for Mrs. Tandemschnocker," I lied, "and I don't know where to start." I sighed as deeply as I could to make sure she believed me.

"Pomes, huh?" she said softly.

"Po-ems!" I corrected firmly, remembering the many times Mrs. Tandemschnocker had made us repeat the word after her. Even though we were the only ones on the road, I looked around to see if anyone had heard. It was embarrassing to hear her say 'pomes' exactly the way Mrs. Tandemschnocker had told us not to say it. For a moment I wished if Nana couldn't look like Carly, she could at least talk like Mrs. Tandemschnocker.

"Oh?" she said, surprised. She relaxed a little and ran her hand in a quick brush through her hair. "I thought something that needed some real figgering out was what was lonesoming you, but if that's all it is, then it's nothing. Let's you and me stop here for a minute and figger this out before we continue this climb." She stopped and stretched her hand out across my rut to stop me.

Aside from laughter that embarrassed me and using words I didn't understand, it seemed like she was always figgering out something.

"Figure out? What's there to figure out?" I asked, pushing through her hand and continuing on. "There is nothing to figure out." I pronounced the word as carefully and as clearly as I could each time, hoping she could learn from me how to say it correctly. She ignored my question and continued after me.

"Has your teacher ever talked to you about poetry?"

"Yes, all week. She said we had to write at least five poems."

"Well, pomes and poetry are not quite the same thing. Did she tell you that?"

"No. What's the difference?"

"A pome is no more poetry than a pomer is a poet."

"What's a pomer?"

"Well, if a farmer farms and a baker bakes, what do you think a pomer is?"

My eyes met Nana's.

"That's right. You say Mrs. Tandemschnocker didn't explain the difference?"

"No, but she did say that because last year it had been so hot so late into the season, the leaves this year would go from green straight to the ground and not turn red. She said this next term we won't be going on our writing trip to the mountains."

Nana picked up her pace, looked across to my track, and studied me as she walked. Then she stepped out of her track and onto the weeds that separated us. Her tongue moved slowly across her lips as it did when she was figuring things out. Suddenly, she burst out laughing.

"So that's what's bothering you!" she exclaimed. "That this year the leaves will go from green to ground and there will be no gold!" She appeared relieved.

Her laughing voice reminded me of the one she used after tasting the first fruit for sweetness before she pronounced the tree ripe to pick.

"I thought there were some real grasshoppers bothering you," she said, slapping her apron from where it floated ahead of her and bringing it down against her knees. "So that's what's bothering you!" she repeated, flinging her apron back into air position before her. "Well, I don't know much about pomes, but poetry, now that's something different!"

In her excitement, she picked up the pace. Her legs caught up with the floating apron in front of her and she became entangled in the furls of many roses.

"Poetry!" Nana's voice rang with the sparkle of spring when she dropped the first seeds into the garden and talked about the first fruits later on. "Poetry does not live in a house called a pome, you know."

Hearing the forbidden word I looked around once again. How I wished that if she couldn't talk like Mrs. Tandemschnocker at least she would know enough to stop saying 'pome.'

"Do you want to know what the difference is? Come on, let's climb."

Mounds of Light

Nana stepped off the weedy-green down into my track and adjusted her steps to mine.

"Well, a pome is words, and that's all it is."

Her voice dropped off immediately as if it had dipped underground and died. I looked up at her through the silence hoping for more of an explanation. She remained quiet through my perplexion without uttering another word as if silence were explanation enough. Then, with a sudden burst, her voice rang upward as if with new power.

"But poetry!" she exclaimed in a different voice and weaving her fingers through the air. "Poetry is sudden lightning that hits the heart for one instant and is gone!"

Her eyes grew big and shiny. For a moment she sparkled in my direction, then continued.

"I remember when I was your age, how fascinated I was by fire in the sky! Still am. Those enormous clouds started up by just being faint mist. Then they bunched up and went to arguing, puffing themselves out against each other until they became thick. All day under the sun they simmered. By evening they had boiled themselves dark. So black they were, they stood out thick and lumpy against the night. My lord, how they churned and stormed against each other! Sounded just like God rolling wagonload after wagonload of sinners across an old wood bridge!"

In her excitement, Nana walked no longer looking down, but up, as she streaked her hands into each other. I could see blue through the weave of her fingers.

"Every now and then those enormous billows turned into mounds of light that blew up from the inside out. I laid in bed wondering how so much darkness could hold in that much light. How could so much fire splash about without damaging the sky? The night would settle down for a few moments. Then, suddenly, I would hear a crrrrrackling flash, and a very quick, electric man made of many lines appeared in the black!"

She charged her fingers back and forth into each other gathering greater blue between them.

"Powerful he was. For a special instant the whole earth shined with light. Even the veins on the cottonwood leaves outside my window stood out. The brilliant man walked around for an instant, then, almost in that same flash, he was pulled back up into the clouds. His light was."

She tossed both hands upward and brought them down empty.

"Another man appeared. Twisted light. Immediately, the darkness swallowed him. Soon, other men, twins even, were born from inside the light. Many, many men in the darkness, actually."

She turned from her fingers and looked at me.

"But you know what? To this day I have never seen two exactly alike. And only seldom do I see them walking together, even when their lightning happens at the same moment and from the same branch of thunder. Have you?"

I remained quiet, unable to see what lightning men had to do with poems for Mrs. Tandemschnocker.

"That's what poetry is, lightning! Different gods fighting in the same place with beautiful weapons!"

"That's not what Mrs. Tandemschnocker...."

God Looking Down

"Poetry is God looking down," Nana continued excitedly without hearing my interruption, "and how He looks down on what He looks down and when! And there is so much He sees that you can't pen it up in a pome. Such as when I was a child."

Nana looked deep into the sky and went far away in her eyes.

"I remember one night, how it was, full of dreams. All night the coyotes kept following me from one dream to another, biting off moon with every howl. The following morning when I woke up, I looked to the pale of the eastern lines, and to my sadness, there the round light was, poor thing, disappearing into a lesser and lesser slice. I was so startled. 'Look!' I cried. 'The moon is ruined!' Everyone looked at me strange and laughed."

Nana came back into her eyes, looked down into mine, and laughed her half-laugh again.

"Poetry," she said, winking. "Maybe we don't have to go to the mountain to find it."

"I don't understand. How can the moon be ruined? It was just a dream and so were the coyotes."

"Are you sure? The moon maybe is a dream because it is so high, but what about dream coyotes that go from one eye to the other in the night howling?"

Nana winked.

A Queen Comes Calling

"Another time I remember answering the telephone and the woman's voice was so beautiful I immediately saw her face. You should have seen how my heart floated when I saw her in my mind. I knew right away I was talking to a queen."

Nana's hands went from making lightning to being very quiet. She clasped them together and brought them to her breast. Then she opened them slowly, as if a book crowded with mystery.

"The queen's voice was so gentle, I knew she had to be part garden air and her dress bits of bloom from every flower. Oh, she was so beautiful on the telephone!"

"Like a glass doll?"

Nana must have seen my sudden interest because she laughed and burst open even more.

"Yes! Like a reflection on glass, like a princess sleeping inside a marble! Before hanging up, the queen said she would be over the next day. How I waited all morning for her to appear. Finally, about midday there was a knock at the door. I opened it and there she was, an old woman who was my grandmother's best friend. My heart came apart for a moment and floated down like a plume from a disappearing bird, but then went very high when she opened a small box and pulled out bread she had baked for us. The aroma in that box was air more beautiful than the picture of her voice in my mind."

Nana breathed in deeply.

"Oh, my!" she exclaimed. "The bread old people can make!"

Nana satisfied her hunger with air.

"Now that's poetry," she said simply. "What do you think?"

"The princess inside the marble, maybe," I said, knowing for certain that old women and smelling bread was not what Mrs. Tandemschnocker expected from us.

"Poetry is anything that splinters into your heart for an instant like glass and then everything waters back together when you pull your finger out. After the needle is in you, your heart gets used to it and hope comes back because, if you let it, your heart can eat up needles."

Old women, bread, and hearts eating needles? No. I was sure of what Mrs. Tandemschnocker would do if I turned in a paper with that.

"Poetry," Nana continued, "can also be the great fear you feel when you see a blind man trusting his cane in heavy traffic with the same calm lean he uses while in the park alone."

Nana closed her eyes and poked about in blindness.

"In dread for him you watch as he pokes along, knowing that at each tap he's going to crash into someone."

She opened them in my direction.

"But just as it never happens in the park because he has memorized the trees, it never happens among people either because what's really happening is a miracle moving through the crowd. He never bumps into anyone. In fact, after he's gone, you hear a commotion where he disappeared. Someone has bumped into him because they were running behind."

Old Shoe

"Can poetry be a person? Like somebody beautiful, I mean?"

"Oh, that's the best kind of poetry, a person. Or how you feel about them maybe. It can even be joy going to sadness then back to joy again."

Nana looked at me, noticed my interest, and jumped on it to feed it.

"The good trembling a little boy like you feels, for example."

"That can be poetry?" I asked, hopefully.

"Oh, absolutely! It's poetry when he feels it crawling all over him."

"It is?" I exclaimed.

"Oh, yes! His fishing pole jerks suddenly downward in the heart of his hand and he pulls back with all his might until his body and pole become two half circles. Then, sadness overwhelms the little fisher when all he brings up is an old shoe. Imagine catching a useless shoe, and losing your worm on top of that!"

"Oh, fish," I muttered, as flatly as I could. "Where's the joy in that?"

Tiny lightning hit Nana's eyes. "Good question! As he threads his hook through the heart of a fresh worm, gladness becomes the greater again when he looks at the crumpled hulk he tossed aside on the grassy bank. There the poor shoe lies. Quiet, resting, the tongue no longer wagging. From that moment on, the little man is a wise fisherman because he knows the old leather will not have to tumble in the current anymore. Can you imagine shivering under water forever like an old, lost shoe?"

"Yes," I nodded, faking her out, wondering how anyone could feel sorry for an old shoe, but imagining even better everyone's laughter when I added an old shoe to the needle-eating heart of the old bread woman that made up Mrs. Tandemschnocker's list.

"Poetry can even be a woman's dress when it swirls in a special

19

way."

"Can it be anything they wear, like earrings?" I asked again with renewed hope.

"Oh, absolutely! Remember when you told me how some of the other students might like school a little better if Mrs. Tandemschnocker was a little different? Well, I'm sure she is aware of that. You recall how just yesterday you said she was starting to become a little more friendly?"

"Yes."

"Well, I'll be willing to bet one morning not too long ago her dress felt that special swirl."

"How?"

"Midway to her morning table, I am sure she twirled around and changed directions in her heart and went directly to her cupboard."

"Why?"

Nana halted, held one arm out and brought me to a stop. Looking into my eyes, she punctuated the air with one finger held high like Mrs. Tandemschnocker before an important test. "Because at that moment she decided she wanted to be a nicer teacher. So you know what she did? She reached into her cupboard, walked back to her coffee and put in all ten lumps of sugar in that bitter black even if it did make her a little fat!"

Ladder to heaven

Nana laughed and brought her finger down. A wrinkle winked from the corner of her eye. I smiled as Mrs. Tandemschnocker in her long, dark dress, ten lumps larger than she really was, came into my mind.

"Come," Nana motioned with her lesson finger, "let's rest a minute."

Pulling me off the gravel track and walking a short distance through a small clump of trees, she then guided me to the edge of the stream that fed our well. She stopped under the large oak where she and I had built my treehouse and in whose enormous trunk gnarls I played forts and castles. I looked at the two long poles we planted deep on either side of some flat stones, then at the old boards we nailed as steps between the poles. My eyes followed the ladder upward. Somewhere high in the thicket of leaves the two poles came together. Hidden in the green sunlight among the lengths of curvy-edged leaves I could see the scraps of lumber and dead branches that formed the floor and walls of my kingdom. At the foot of the huge tree, the small stream tumbled over several large boulders. As the current washed over the rocks, it rounded itself over their smooth faces, thinning itself into many sheets of light that flowed through the underbrush.

Nana sat on the lowest step of the ladder while I leaned on the pole beside her.

"Remember when we plundered the Old Place so we could build this empire?" she asked, tapping the old corral slat on which she sat.

"Yes."

"These poles remind me of kiva poles."

"What are kiva poles?"

"Kivas are sacred holes in the earth where Indians pray. They are holy. They use poles like these to make ladders so they can climb back up to the sun. And these flagstones, couldn't have done it without Grampo," she added, stomping the solid slabs of rock Grandpa and his brother Cesario helped break apart and haul from the abandoned fireplace to support the beams. "Foursquare strong, they are."

"What does that mean?"

"Foursquare strong means can't tumble and won't give. Steps are set just right too, look. Any little old lady could climb these."

Closing one eye and cocking her head slightly, Nana rested her chin on the step above her. For a long minute she gazed upward long between the poles.

"Yeppers," she finally said, with the same firm voice she used when all was well in her garden or when every egg under Top Feathers had turned into a chick. "We took the best poles off that old sheep pen. Look at that! Looks just like a ladder to heaven, don't it? Yeppers, it does. Just look at it."

I looked at the weathered boards we had stripped from the rabbit hutches and nailed between the sheep poles as they climbed evenly, shiny gray on top, shady dark underneath.

Nana squinted as she peered upward though the thicket of leaves into the kingdom.

"A few rabbit gnaws here and there going up, but my lord, what a beautiful house when you get there! Look how those leaves lace everything together up high. What God can do with some old boards, a little air, common sky, and a cloud or two. Even those old rusty nails we pulled out of the chicken coop are bent silver in the sun. What a mansion!"

Nana patted the tree's trunk.

"And these old oaks, don't let nothing stop them. See how the bark corkscrews round and round up? This poor thing has been twisting itself up out of the earth in this spot for at least a hundred years. Ground can get pretty tight around anything that wants to grow, you know."

She glanced in my direction for a moment, then back to the ladder where she rested her chin on the step once again. With her eyes, she climbed the kiva poles step by step. Reaching the top, they went all around the treehouse and stepped inside. She gazed on every old board as though it were a strange new flower that had suddenly appeared in her garden. She greeted every rusty nail with the same nod she had used during the final hammer blow to drive it.

For a moment, I remembered Nana, aproned in the high leaves, walking among the green, placing plank to branch, and nailing, nailing, nailing. Nailing for me. I remembered her last nail and the final pound. Tossing the hammer down, she emerged from the magical castle like a king's fairy-tale slave. Step by step she descended backward until she stood on the stones. Turning around slowly she adjusted her apron and faced me. Then, like the boss fairy who has sent the other workers home so she can get every ounce of credit and the king's attention on top, she stood tall beside the ladder. She cleared her throat and, giving her apron a special sail, she bowed low and proudly announced, "Your palace, your Highness, is finished."

"Yep. Times is now and again when earth crowds in hard."

Nana's voice interrupted my king thoughts as she lifted her head off the slat that led to heaven. She bounced her weight on the staircase, but the treehouse limb failed to move. She lifted herself higher a second time and landed solidly on the second of heaven's steps. The treehouse, perched like a stickery magpie nest on the limb, barely trembled in the quaking of the huge oak's leaves.

"Rumbles a little, don't it?"

A third time she lifted herself and slammed back down against the plank.

"But she ain't coming down."

Settling herself satisfied on the slat, she continued. "Yup. Only odds and ends nailed a little here and tucked there against the tree for a branch to hold, that's how you build a house in the air. And this is a perfect spot. Look at that small waterfall breaking over those rocks. Little river here seems to be unspooling itself downstream forever, don't it."

Nana rose from her seat on heaven's ladder and, slowly, as if tasting the cool grass with her feet, dragged them toward the grassy bank at the edge of the tumbling water. With the caution old Top Feathers used when settling on her eggs, she carefully pushed aside several blooms.

"Daisies," she said, nestling herself in the yoke-yellow and white.

Without removing her shoe, she dipped her foot into the never-ending water. The river split into many flashes and wrapped itself around her ankle, but didn't stop its flow. As the current journeyed downstream, it carried in its ripples the many shadows her leg kept dropping into the water.

"Water's good here, too," she said, after a long pause, dipping her other foot. She reached one arm outward and swept it over the grass in a circle around her. Raking several plants into her hand, she examined them. Then, with the other she carefully plucked the stems of their leaves and laid them on her apron. When she had gathered a small heap, she displayed them in my direction. "Do you know what these are?"

"No."

"Come sit down beside me," she directed.

Putting the leaves and bits of different grasses almost under my nose, she once again offered me her open palm.

"Up close, do you know what these are?"

"No," I repeated, hoping she wouldn't tell me they were good to eat and that we would have to start picking them.

She singled out a long, jagged leaf.

"This is poleo. Very good for colds. Actually, very good for whatever ache you want ridded of. Even makes a good minty tea to just sit and enjoy."

She separated a small leaf that looked like an open hand made of tiny lace and mashed it between her fingers. "Oshá. This is called oshá. Nothing better for flu. Here, smell it."

I leaned into her thumb and finger. The sharp smell of the brown-green leaf grabbed deep into my nose.

"Yuck! Smells like flu, alright!"

Laughter sprang into Nana's face when she saw my grimace, but in the same instant, it vanished.

"What do you know about flu?" she asked, almost seriously. Then, almost as if not wanting me to respond, she answered herself.

"Yes, it does smell like flu."

She touched her face to the leaves and inhaled deeply.

"Yes," she sighed. "You're right. It does smell like flu." She stared at the leaves in her hand, then at me for a moment.

"I have a check plus in health," I said, quickly.

"That's good," she replied, a smile returning to her face. She pointed out another smelly leaf.

"This one is oregano. Very healthy for you as well," she instructed, "but I can tell you there's something even healthier."

"What's that?" I asked, wondering what stink she was going to harvest next.

"Crying. The healthiest thing I've ever done in my life is cry. Sponges can hold in only so much water, then you have to wring them out."

"What do you mean?"

Nana ignored my question and instead picked up another leaf.

"And this little, stick-looking thing is cota."

Nana labeled with strange names the remaining leaves and pronounced them all good.

"These were the only remedies we had when I was a girl. We used to gather as many different plants as we could during the growing part of the year for the dead times like winter. Wonderful remedies. Indian remedies, all of them, from before our time. Powerful as an Indian's prayer, too, people used to say."

She looked up at the treehouse, down at the stream, then slowly around the oak at the many different plants growing in its shade.

"Yep! This is a good place. When remedies grow wild, you can bet your bones the water's good, too."

"What does remedies mean?"

"Medicine. Man has many diseases," she said. "Some are simple and will just go away by themselves. Others, he has to use remedies like these. Some diseases, like grasshoppers, just keep on making and laying eggs that go forever. It doesn't matter what you drink to wash them in or what you plaster together to suffocate them under, you can't break their shells. They just hook both legs on and wave their horns at you."

Nana put her finger into her palm and swirled the leaves slowly as if mixing them into new medicine. She pressed her hand shut then opened it, and smelled the small, tight wad.

"Life was hard back then.." she said, her voice trailing off.

Leaving her words suspended in the air, she turned her attention to tossing the handful of medicine into the stream. As the green ball hit the water and broke apart, every leaf boarded a separate wave and slowly floated away. Nana watched quietly as the water took everything, shadows and all, around the rocks, and finally, downstream. The remedies gone, she gathered her thoughts from the whirlpools of the stream and returned to the words she had left hanging in the air.

"...Oh, we bumped and lumped along, but life was very good."

25

The Best Poetry

Nana pointed to a drying puddle near the edge of the water.

"See these tracks? Skunk. Good poetry leaves good tracks in a person, too. Tracks are the best books if you know how to read them. They can tell you how animals walk."

"How do you know they're skunk?"

"I just do. Tracks along the sand can be cleaned away and you can start all over again after the waves lap up and clean them. But in puddles like this where no water comes, mold just grows thicker as the water gets less and less. Finally, everything dries up and the way the animal walked stays forever. Walking on mud is pretty permanent."

"I still don't see how you know they are skunk."

Nana took her finger and, rubbing it over the prints, turned them to sand.

"Skunk or not, there's fresh ground now. And tracks can be poetry, too. Even skunk's. Poetry is really nothing more than making good tracks with your mind."

She pointed to a glen on a nearby hill.

"You see how that grove of cottonwoods rocks and sways gently over there because it's spring? Later this year when God gives his great fall cry that will take us from summer through autumn into winter, those very same trees will hear His many winds come up through the gulches and they will tremble. Quake and toss they will, I am sure, not knowing how His gusts will bend them. That's going to be some nice poetry. We'll have to see if we can make some time to come up here and watch Him."

"Does God have to be in a poem?"

"No, and most of the time He is no where to be found in pomes, but He always is in poetry because, like I told you, poetry is God looking down. Sometimes He looks down bending over the world in a rainbow. Sometimes He does it in the weeping willow. I told you that last year, during those heavy rains after the long heat when the grasshoppers were feasting my poor garden to death, remember?"

"I remember. And there were rainbows in the sky all day. Do you remember?"

"I remember," Nana replied, placing her hand lightly on my arm. "That was beautiful poetry, those bending stripes all over the blue. Did you think that was poetry?"

Nana answered for me.

"I'm sure you did. But you know, to me the best poetry of my life has been me walking where God can watch me. Such as in a forest hungry once and stumbling upon a berry. It was the littlest of berries, moritas de San Juan, we used to call those tiny plumpies, Saint John's berries. They grow right next to the ground, right off the stalk on a very short runner so you have to be looking. I reached down, picked that little red, and mmmm! I remember looking up through the canopy of leaves and saying, 'It was delicious, God, because there was no hand between your hand and my hand when you gave it, only my tongue.' Do you understand?"

"What's a canopy."

"Canopy is anything that covers."

Dancing on the Grape

Nana pulled her apron up, edged closer over the bank, and dipped both feet knee-deep into the stream.

"And what about water? Do you like it?"

"Of course I like water," I said, wondering why anyone would even think about such a simple thing as water.

"Do you see those men down there?"

I followed Nana's finger into the distance and the tiny people in the valley below.

"Migrants. Mano Mucio is probably among them. He's sixty five already. Much too old to be working like that."

Nana squinted to see if she could see her friend, then, shaking her head, she said, "Poetry can be migrants harvesting a field in the great heat of the day, too. They are luckier than many of us. You know why?"

"Why?"

"Because at lunch they get to catch the sun when they tip their glass and it rainbows for a moment tinkling. A lot of people don't know that water tastes its bestest when you're thirsty, you know. Another thing they don't know about common water is that it doesn't have one vitamin of food, but you can't live without it. We are water in the world, someone told me once, our bodies."

I glanced once again at the many colored dots scattered throughout the far fields. Some harvested in one direction, while others, scattered snails under the sun, picked in the opposite.

"Nana, I don't know what very many words mean, so how can I write poetry? What are migrants?"

"Migrants means people moving around working and working until one day they move on and then you don't see them anymore. And look how the different fields patch out in every direction. The whole valley makes me think of a huge basket filled with odd breads that God feeds His different people. Don't you think?"

"If that's true, He's baked some fields more than others," I added, noticing the different shades of brown.

"Well, that could be. When I look out and see migrants, they remind me that to harvest our food, we have to walk on it."

"Walk on our food?"

"Yes, its simple to see. Our shoe is always on the wheat. First, we hold it steady with our foot so's we can sickle it. A sickle is that curvy half-moon knife hanging in the wood shed. Then, after cutting it, when we gather up the fallen grains, we walk on the poor thing again. But that's poetry too because wheat always leads to life."

I must have appeared confused about people walking on food because Nana continued.

"God has decided that. And then comes the grinding when He turns it into flour."

Nana made a fist and began hitting it into the open palm of her other hand.

"Crush the corn to make a meal! Trudge the wheat to make your bread! Pound the milk to make your butter!"

Nana crashed her palms together several more times, then threw up her hands and said simply, "That is how man eats."

A smile came over her face.

"But that's what makes life delicious, pounding your own milk."

"Like the berry in the woods?"

"Yes! Like the berry in the woods! Better, because like a good father who has not forgotten the child in his man, God also has him dancing on the grape to get his wine."

"How come those migrants don't..."

Nana interrupted immediately.

"We are all migrants."

The Antlers of Man

"There's one thing you should know about migrants who don't think they are," Nana continued. "Some become so accustomed to their land they come to love it more than the food it gives them."

She pointed toward the fields.

"You can't tell it from here, but every one of those fields has a fence around it. Sometimes the fences grow right along with the crops they hold in. I saw it once. You can learn an absolute lot about migrants who don't think they are by studying their fences. They start them out, their fences, with a small scratch on the ground, a little line. They care for them, turning them into tiny borders around a flower garden. Plants in, weeds and grasses out, you know. Next thing you know, they are making borders out of driftwood, crooked sticks, upside-down bottles and odd slats. You can use almost anything you find for fencing when you want to separate the species."

"What does species mean?"

"Species means kinds and sorts. It can be kinds of flowers or all sorts of animals. Anything can be used to separate and keep apart. Greenery, small plants, April bells. I've seen entire neighborhoods hedged off behind bleeding hearts. They bloom in blood. The red is always dangling in the white."

"You mean the flowers?"

"Yes. Like the ones I have under the kitchen window, beside the daisies. Many people even go to the mountains and uproot entire shrubs like the wild summer rose and transplant them into their yards to make their hedges. In winter, their thorns make barb wire, the city kind."

"What are April bells?"

"They are flowers, but of course they don't ring. Many times, a hedge is not tall enough, so people will build a fence. Old tires half buried, black rainbows in the ground they are. Fences of glass and rock, empty apple crates, crooked sticks sticking up, even. Fences can be chains linked together, or wrought. I once saw an antler fence."

"What is wrought?"

"Wrought means iron pounded in a forge and beaten by the smith. The smiths use all kinds of metal to fence people out. Or their things in. The flowers in their picture windows are iron, and they usually put tin leaves on their doors. Many people prefer walls over hedges and fences because they last much longer."

Nana paused and looked again in the direction of the little people. "Tiny, aren't they?" she said.

"Yes."

"Going everywhere, but always staying on. Some of those fields down there have walls around them," Nana continued. "Many even with crushed glass on top. Those walls have been in the family for generations. Rocks the grandfather picked up along the way or maybe gathered from the mountainside. Paid for them with heave and hoist, like they say."

"What's heave and hoist?"

"That's not caring how heavy something is, you just go ahead and lift it, and take it with you. You may have left a bone behind, but you got your rock. Once he has whatever stones he likes, he carries them along until he comes to the place where he thinks his line should be. There he lays them down like his father taught him. Muds them into place. Fathers teach wall-building to their sons. They add their own rocks to the heap and their own mud. And so it goes, everybody carrying rocks on down the line. And mud."

Nana looked at me for a moment, then she continued.

"Even babies, I've seen them. Can't go beyond their first few steps when they start reaching down and putting pebbles in their mouths. Later, they fill their pockets. 'Magic stones' they call the prettier ones. Like that one there."

Nana reached down and pulled out a smooth river rock stuck to the bank.

"See this curvy part? Looks like a fairy's cave. Kind of magical, isn't it? And this chipped edge, it could be a cliff where dragons live. It's hard to break children of the rock habit. But if you don't, they just keep on picking up bigger and bigger ones. By the time they grow old, what started out magic ends up being a wall cathedral-high and churchyard-thick. Enormous structures that refuse to budge. Some stones become part of the family, come alive, even. And you can't yank them up because the roots go all the way back to the yester, like they say. Yester means something that we don't understand because it happened in the long, long ago. Like that horn fence I mentioned."

"The antler fence?"

"Yes. When I first saw it, it even hurt me a little to see it so pokey between the two homes. I'd never seen so many bones growing together, sticking out everywhere. The whole thing was nothing but points. Some years later I happened to go by again, and you won't believe it, but the wall had sprouted new horns. It was also taller and went completely around one of the houses, even on the roof. The owner of the house was a hunter. He came out and began watering his flowers. Seeing how the fence had grown from when I had first seen it, made me think that splashed water had made his horns grow. Poor man's dirt always yields abundant fences, people used to say. I guess you could say that a fence is the only crop that grows without the least manuring."

"Nana, sometimes you use a lot of words I don't understand."

"That's just how some people used to talk back then. But you don't have to know the dictionary way of words before you can write poetry, you know. Well, for pomes maybe you do because pomes are just words put together. But I don't know. I haven't been trained to pome. For poetry, the main thing you have to know is the natural way of words. You learn this by listening to people. Sanctuary, for example. Do you know what that means?"

"No."

Nana pulled one leg from the water, then the other. She ran her hands slowly back and forth across her shin to dry it. Like a little girl playing with her favorite doll, she watched as the sun dried the water and turned her glassy leg brown.

"Come," she said, wringing the hem of her apron, "let's move around to the other side of the tree, away from the breeze."

On her hands and knees, Nana crawled around the tree, pulling her apron out from under her as she went to keep her knees from stepping on it. I followed on all fours, keeping my eye on her wet soles dragging through the flowers. She crawled away from the stream and sat down with her back against the oak.

"What do you feel right now? Do you still feel breeze?"

"Barely."

"What you are feeling is sanctuary. I don't know what the dictionary says, but sanctuary is being in a quiet spot in March like now where the wind isn't blowing, and there is only sun around you."

"Nana, you have never talked this way before."

"Perhaps I have... maybe you just haven't noticed?"

Her voice rose at the end, and what started out an explanation ended up a question.

"Arteests"

Nana patted the ground beside her.

"Move over here closer."

Holding my back against the tree, I twisted around until I found a comfortable spot near her.

"Poetry is really God breathing. His breath on things, I mean. Here," she said, patting a clump of moss on the trunk beside her, "lean against this. See how cool it feels?"

I moved in closer, against her.

"Yes, His breath," she started out again. "But, we have to notice to see it. It's there. It's there, I know. And once we see it, we can see that poetry can be God having fun, too. I'm sure of that."

"Do you think God has fun?"

"Oh, I am certain of it! Like when He looks down on those bearded artists who apron themselves in paint and cap their heads with those half-loaf looking caps. Like this."

Nana pretended to cock an invisible cap off to one side of her head.

"Of course they don't call themselves painters, but 'arteests.' They think those silly looking piles of wool atop their heads make them special and that wearing them half off their head makes them even more specialer. I've seen them going about thinking they can float above everything they paint. Like this."

Nana gave her head a quick strut like Top Feathers when the crusty thing grew all her spring feathers back.

"There they stand, holding their flat wooden hands, fingernailed with nine messy colors as they try to paint an angel on a flat white cloth."

Nana put her hand on my knee, and pressing hard, stood up. She took a couple of steps, and stopped directly in front of me. Spreading her hand palm up, she puffed out her chest. Then, swashing her hand in front of her, she painted the air.

"Like this," she repeated. "They put a little swish, swish here, and they daub a little swash, swash there on what's supposed to be an angel. Then, taking a step backward, the wool-heads cock themselves this-a-way and they cock themselves that-a-way like very proud roosters as they admire their work with a squinty eye. But then, without the lop-capped cocks knowing it, God walks up quietly behind them, looks over the shoulders of the half-loafs at what has ended up being nothing more than the picture of little man with the face of a child and wings. Because of all the feathers in their crow, the half-caps can't hear God laughing right in their ears."

I laughed.

"God shakes his head as He thinks out loud in his god-voice. 'Arteests?' He says to Himself with a chuckle. 'Ha! And to think poor children whose only toy is snow can fall down on any bank, flap their arms every which way like a sparrow dying, and make angels that can actually vanish.' That's what God says."

"Nana," I challenged, somewhat upset to think that God would laugh at anybody, "I don't think God laughs at people!"

"Oh, God isn't laughing at the arteests, silly! He's only laughing at their angels. I'm sure if we could see God's face, we would see compassion. Compassion means feeling very good to people."

"Compassion?"

"Yes, that's what's in God's heart when He looks down into the baby peacock naked in the stickery nest. Nothing can be uglier on earth than a poor, baby bird with its ugly, triangle mouth wide open begging through the skin of its eyes. But you must remember that in time, God will dress that naked sight with the feathers He has chosen to color it the bird of paradise."

This World Does Not Hold its Color

"Sometimes poetry is inside us, too," Nana continued. "I feel it when my knees hurt more from kneeling as I ask God to forgive me, than my heart does over what I shouldn't have done in the first place. What do you think?"

"I guess."

"And poetry can also be when a person wonders."

"About what?"

"Oh, anything. Time, the seasons, their color. This is especially true about people of the earth who watch time come and go, like planters."

"You mean farmers?"

"Yes. They go by a different clock. Their almanac is the colors around them."

"What's a amlanac?"

"Almanac, you mean? An almanac is when people look up at the stars and other things that happen in the sky that tell them when to put their seeds in the ground. Everything that moves around up there tells them what to do down here, like plant or cut weeds from their sap so they won't come back again. Farmers can even tell from looking up when they have worked enough to sit under their trees to enjoy the coming plums. And the nuts, too. They sit alone, but sometimes you get two or three of them under a flowered branch."

"I've seen you under the peach tree."

"Oh, but my favorite is sitting in the blossom of the apple! I am the flower of the world, I tell you, when I can sit beside an apple bloom."

Nana clapped her hands together with the joy of a girl who has just heard her princess doll talk back.

"But as I was saying, when you get two or three of them under the same tree, all they do is talk time in color. In spring they say, 'Summer comes to paint the flower.' In summer, all you hear is 'Sugar this and sugar that.'"

"What do you mean?"

"Well, they are talking of sugar time, fall, when the fruit swells watery and the soft nut pushes with all its sweetness out and wins against the wooden shell. Then comes winter, when they sit quiet beside their fires, usually alone, because everyone is busy making sure they don't go out. Barely touching the quiet flames, they strip the rind and begin to separate the flesh."

"What does...."

"Rind is skin," Nana interrupted, as if having read my mind. "They pluck the fruit, the nuts, until the bone is bare and all the world is white. Late into the night they tend the flame, but none have power over sleep that calls. Everyone has to leave his fire. Shells, ash is all that's left of flame, skin shriveling alongside the dying ember. Or husks maybe, gently rocking where they fell, little boats waiting for a passenger. With fire losing life and everyone in bed, all you hear going from hearth to hearth is tiny flames growing fainter, fainter calling out, 'This world does not hold its color.'"

"What do they mean by that?"

"I guess it's like colored pencils. Eventually, the color runs out, and we have to go back to lead. I'm sure you've wondered about the color in pencils."

"No, Nana, I have never wondered about pencils. What's there to wonder? Red ones write red and blue ones blue."

"Yes, but what about the other end? Do red erasers erase red and blue blue?"

"Nana, who cares about erasers!"

"Exactly! Most people go right to the point and miss out on possibilities. How many people you know have ever taken the time to notice that even the blackest eraser erases clear. It's the same when farmers and people of the earth erase. Everything goes to clear. Color don't matter to the eraser."

Nana pointed to a flower with her foot.

"Even these dead dandelions. Look."

Reaching into the green, she plucked out an empty head without breaking the bubble fuzz. Then, puffing barely on the fluff, she said, "See? It don't take hardly nothing to send ashes parachuting off into the gray."

"Why do farmers need a amlanac? Everyone knows you plant in the springtime."

"Almanac, you say? Well, springtime is different from spring

36

time, you know. Spring is not in March or April, but when the first bird of the year sings. I discovered this when still very young. The best spring I ever had was one year in February."

"Spring in February?"

"Oh, my lord, yes!" Nana exclaimed.

She clasped both hands on her lap, cradled them tight between her legs, and closed her eyes. She looked up and, smiling, rocked gently back and forth. She appeared asleep, remembering.

She opened her eyes again and looked at me.

"Birds don't sing in the dark, you know, much less in winter nights. That cold morning I had barely awakened with the covers tight in my fist and my fist tight to my chin. Houses back then were so drafty, especially after the fires went out. Heat going out one crack just sucked in cold through a sister crack."

Nana jerked her shoulders a little and shivered.

"Anyway, I knew there was no reason to get up. The dead trees would still be there, bony gray as always and all around, holding everything scared. Reminded me of a skeleton with a million ribs holding in a beating heart. Suddenly—and even now I can barely believe it, because the day was still far from appearing—I heard a bird in the dark morning! In my excitement, I flung off the covers, jumped into my shoes, and rushed to open the door. Nothing moved outside, but after hearing the song, I refused to go back to bed. 'Where there's a song, there's a bird,' I told myself, 'and where there's a bird, there's spring.' I waited. That February cold was coming into the house all around me, but I didn't mind it. Finally, I saw a small gray wren, no color to it—ugly as the sky, actually—but still a bird. And then came spring!"

Nana's eyes lit up.

"When that winter wren hopped to another branch, it took with it another bird I hadn't seen! The second bird took with it another as it followed the first, and soon the dead wood came to life. It was a chain pulling itself out of the gray. I tell you, that dawning was filled with flight! I was so excited my feet were tingling. Then, I looked down and found out why. I had put my shoes on the wrong foot."

Nana laughed out loud at her own story.

I could think of many other things I would rather do to amuse myself besides standing naked in the cold and looking at gray birds, but I laughed anyway.

"Oh, we still had snow and ice for a long time after that," she continued, "because May, when the sun flowers, and June, when the air smells like one big apple, both were still three months away according to the calendar. But not for me, not for me! That almanac wren told me spring had come."

Angel in the Distance

Nana was quiet for a few minutes, her eyes looking far away while she continued tasting February spring.

"My," she said as if talking to herself, "how the cold came in through those houses back then and penned itself inside with us all winter long." Then, as if noticing I was beside her, she pointed.

"Look as far as you can. How far can you see?"

"The sky, I guess."

"Yes, the sky. That can be pretty far for some people, you know, but what we call distance can actually be quite near. And that can be poetry, too. The blacksmith who sharpens my hoe, for example. Every time I take it to him, before I reach his forge, I stop and watch him from the hill. There he is low in the little valley inside his distant shop looking more like some dark animal—a bear groping inside its cave, perhaps—than a man. His sledge is going up and down in constant ringing, inging! inging! on the anvil."

Nana pounded the air with a pretend hammer while her mouth made the metal sound.

"If I didn't know him better, from far away I would think anger ruled his forge. He pounds away with all his might, you know. All those sparks, my goodness! Everyone knows he is a wonderful man at heart, though. Anyway, the last time I took him my hoe, he was pounding outside his forge. I watched as the echoes of his hammer traveled toward me through the smokey distance between us. He pounded and the echoes rang, he pounded and the echoes rang. Pound! Ring!... Pound! Ring!... Pound! Ring!... Then, to my surprise, and this is because we were so far apart and the pounding took a few moments to reach me, the sounds reversed themselves as they crossed the valley. He pounded, and it was on the upswing when his sledge was in the sky tight against a cloud, that I heard his hammer ring. Ring! Pound!... Ring! Pound!... Ring! Pound!"

Later inside his shop when I handed him my hoe, I noticed he had been beating wings for a tin angel. From where he was working, the blacksmith couldn't see it, but I could from a distance. Beside his forge, he was only pounding on a sheet of tin, but there, on the far-away cloud, he was making another angel out of vapor and he didn't even know it."

I tried to imagine sharp tin against a cloud, but Nana interrupted.

"Sometimes poetry is not knowing the answer, too."

"Like on a test, you mean?"

"Yes, but not a paper test. Some things we simply are not supposed to know, and that is very good."

"How can not knowing something be very good?" I asked.

"Sounds a little tangled, don't it?"

I nodded.

"Well, it ain't really, if you stop and follow the threads."

"What do you mean?"

"Well, does anyone know when a pony becomes a horse or when a boy goes into a man? Nobody knows. Or take something even simpler. When does the hole in a jacket become so big, that what's left of the cloth is really parts of a jacket around a hole?"

I Prefer Light

"I still don't understand, Nana. I thought it was good to know everything."

"I don't think so."

Nana leaned toward me, and looked squarely at me.

"Unseen things that cricket blackly in the night solitary and alone, for example, with their black eyes rooted in the dark and waving their little horns. Those are not good to know. I'm sure if you had the misfortune to see one, whatever it is, it would love to tell you its name. But you would find it so terrible you probably wouldn't want to even say it."

"You mean crickets?"

Still pressed in my direction, she replied, "Oh, no. Crickets are fine. I'm talking about things that cricket in the dark. I've never seen them. But I know if you let them, or if you look for them, they will bother your sleep from every corner."

Nana relaxed and leaned back against the trunk as she repeated, "No, no, crickets are fine. They sing with their legs, you know. But you know what, even a cricket, I've never seen one chirping in the daytime. Me, I prefer light, too. Daisies in the sun like God's angels suspended good and barely above the meadow waving white because their hearts are golden. The wind moves them back and forth panning gold while the sun sluices through their petals."

"What is sluices?"

"Sluicing? I think it means people moving dirt back and forth round and round until gold appears."

God is Summer and Winter Put Together

"Nana, why do you talk so much about God?"

Nana laughed and hung on to her laughter a little longer than usual. I noticed how joyful Nana's eyes could be.

"Old women and God have always gone hand in hand," she said, still laughing. "Old men, too, and children. They love Him. I am no different. And I guess if you put all of us together with God, that can be poetry, too. Old people and children are everywhere, you know. And so is He, doing so many things at once all over the earth for everybody because everyone is needing different things at the same time."

"What do you mean?"

"Well, like when He tries to gladden the world after the drizzle of the rain. Maybe you've heard Him at our house. Have you ever listened to how He drips music on that loose piece of tin on the side of the chicken coop? Drop, drop, drop. Have you noticed? You know, where the chickens are always scratching because it is soft?"

"Yes, I always know where the chickens are."

"Well, at the same time that he is gladdening the gutter, He's listening to the ragged farmer down the road complaining as he plows because he wasn't able to save an icicle or two from winter with which to rub away the summer heat. And, while He is doing that, He is also paying careful attention to an ice child in Alaska far away who is wishing for a pocketful of sun from which to pull out a little heat. Over there it's winter. And while God is doing all that, He has to watch all the other children, too, because they are always in the middle."

I remained silent trying to understand how winter and summer could be one.

"Yup. That's God," Nana said to herself, interrupting me as if able to see my thoughts. "That's God alright, summer and winter at the same time, and everything else in between. Actually, if you sit and think about it, God is pretty smart."

42

Angelus

Neither of us said anything for a while. Nana was thinking, looking into the far-away. She sighed low and soft as she always did when figuring things out.

"Poetry can be in silence, too," she said, breaking the quiet. "Many times when people sit silent is when they are talking the loudest, saying the most. Folks don't work as hard nowadays as they did when I was young. I remember going out at sundown—angelus of the evening, we called it—when the migrants gathered around the water trough with their animals before they all went home. Quietly on the water's edge they sat, some standing, in the evening falling orange dust. Every head was hanging. The plow, you know. All day long, they either pulled it or pushed it. Everybody, too tired to talk. Yet, I knew that without a word, everyone was sharing what they all knew, how tired they were. I could smell the horses. Man and animal sharing salt. That's sweat that I remember."

She fell quiet again, then continued.

"But silence can also be a song," she said, her voice more joyful. "If you look closely someday when you are in the meadow, you can see it in the larks. Watch them warble from a distance. You can't hear their song, but you can see it. Their feathers sparkle when the sun cuts into their throats and splashes off."

Of Pigs and Diamonds

Nana removed her wet shoes and, twisting them strongly in her hands, squeezed long, brown trickles from them.

"Poetry teaches many important things that pomes just can't," she said, still looking at the dirty water. "Like diamonds, knowing they are not as good as tasty pig skins when you pull them thick-ringed and curly fresh from the roasting fires."

"I think I would rather have a diamond."

"We all do," she said, laughing. "But what do you think rich people with all those stones curled around their fingers hope for when they get hungry? Maybe when you have everything, a piece of pig is more valuable than a large diamond?"

Again, her voice rose at the end. More and more I was noticing how Nana could take a simple answer and turn it into a question.

Blue Boy

Nana pointed up into the thickness of the oak where a bright orange bird streaked with black and yellow feathers landed on the window sill of the treehouse.

"Oriole, I think," she whispered.

In its mouth was a long thread which it was about to add to its nest.

"A strand he has stolen from one of the neighborhood clotheslines," Nana explained, quietly. Soon, other birds appeared, each with different colored strings.

"Someone is going to be missing a good part of his pajamas," Nana whispered, laughing quietly. "Or worse," she added, opening her eyes wide and making a face. "He's going to have a hole in his sleep!"

I laughed. I liked it when Nana made me laugh.

"With so many wardrobes hanging for the picking on the clotheslines, I wonder what color the first baby bird to be born is going to pick?"

"I don't know, Nana."

"Maybe if its a boy, blue?"

"Blue boy!" I yelled, quietly.

"Yes, and I'm sure he won't be like a couple of animals I know."

"Which ones?" I asked.

I noticed a twinkle in Nana's eyes as she explained.

"The zebra and the magpie. It don't matter what chatter that bird flutters in, or how high the zebra kicks its heels when it gallopzags along, neither one of those two sillies can decide if it wants to be black or white!"

We laughed together.

"Shh. Come on, let's leave them alone. After school is out and you come back this summer, I am sure you will have a new friend in your treehouse."

"I like this place, Nana. I'm glad we built it. Aren't you?"

45

"Oh, yes! Everybody needs a treehouse."

Evening Angel

"Come," said Nana, "let's get on with this climb. Can't go nowhere staying in one place."

"Look, Nana," I said, pointing to our house below, "there's our house way down there, and the grocery tree. We're half-way up the hill."

"Yes," she answered, without looking, "but you can't go forward looking back."

She pulled me onto the path, and pointed upward.

"Can't climb up looking down. Come on."

We came to two large boulders beside the road. Nana stopped, leaned her body against the larger of the rocks, and pointed to the valley below.

"Verdistancia. What a beautiful name for a valley. Look," she said, pointing to a half-plowed field. "There's Mano Manuel and his wife, Mana Vidalia."

Mano Manuel, who took care of the abandoned farm Nana called that old nettle nest, was following his horse behind the plow. Behind him was his wife, matching his every step as she dropped a seed every half-plow length.

"They're such good people to be working that bowl of burrs. I've never seen anyone who works that hard. He was born working, and she was born birthing babies. I think she's midwifed half the people of Verdistancia, and he, cows and horses. He's broked to plow almost every horse in this valley. Been wearing himself smaller and smaller ever since I can remember, grinding that plow all his life through those same stones."

For a while we watched man and horse share the iron point. One pushed while the other pulled.

"I've never heard him complain, either," Nana said. "All's he ever asks for is good weather, it seems. And I've never seen him make a bounty out of that old nettle nest. And yet, every year he leaves the edges of his field unplowed for the pheasants and raccoons. Probably the same little bandits that steal our corn every year, the skunks!"

"But they've never stolen every ear, Nana."

"You're right. Anyway, have you ever noticed how he walks up to that old house of theirs on the hill after plowing?"

"No," I shook my head. "How?"

"Well," she said, resting her body tighter against the boulder, "one of these evenings come out right as the sun is going down and the raccoons out. You'll see him bendy from walking the furrow all day and looking down guiding the plow point. I'm sure he's too tired to even take off his hat. When he reaches the crest of the hill—that's a crest, that little top part of that hill over there—when he reaches the crest in silhouette—silhouette is somebody's thick shadow— when he reaches the crest in silhouette, at the right moment you will see the moon hit his hat just right and turn into a halo. He'll wear the moon until he enters home, then he'll fade into the mist. Just like an evening angel if you could ever see one."

"Does halo mean an angel crown?" I guessed.

"Yes!" Nana exclaimed, with surprised excitement. "That's exactly what it means!"

"I can almost see it, Nana, when you point it out. An old hat can turn into a crown if the moonlight hits it just right!"

"And you don't even have to touch your hat. The light does it all. So now, let me ask you. Is it possible that Mano Manuel has really been wearing a halo all this time, and all we have noticed is his sweaty old felt?"

"Could be. Nana, people say farmers are real wise, especially old ones like him. Are they?"

"Oh, absolutely, but only the ones who put a blade of grass in their mouth."

Nana threw her head back and laughed.

I joined her.

We looked at each other laughing, and laughed even louder.

"Yes, they are wise," Nana said, half in words and half in laughter, "but only up to a point. With their furrows they can stitch a field together using only water. And they can grow more than enough food to feed themselves and their animals, and still have plenty left over to feed even the skunks among us who don't work."

Nana's laughter came to a sudden end. "Skunks!" she repeated, a little irritated.

"But you know what, if all the farmer wisdom was gathered in only one farmer, he still wouldn't be wise enough to know what holds water together. Have you ever thought about that?"

"No."

"Think about it," she said, reaching for my arm. "Come on, let's walk over to the Old Place before we go up any higher."

"Yes! Let's do. I love it there!"

The Old Place

The Old Place was scattered piles of abandoned sheds and buildings where I played fort many times. Whenever any animal strayed from home, it always ended up there, not because the fences were down, but because it was so quiet. Maybe the old chimney stack that rose taller than the ruins was flag enough to call them there. Made of red flagstone with white river rock for base, the tall tower was where a charred crow usually sat spying on everything I did. Maybe he had been there when the house had burned down many years before.

Crawling through the sagging strands of barbs which all the animals ignored, Nana and I walked past the bare spot where the garden had long since been. The ground was still faintly ridged. A few green weeds grew through a tangle of tumbleweeds where once food had bloomed.

"Every draggy-foot cow in the country that finds this place keeps crisscrossing these poor poles back and forth," Nana muttered, as she made her way over several corral poles. "It's a miracle everything isn't kindling by now."

She pointed to a pile of poles.

"Those pens over there were always full of babies this time of year, I remember," Nana said. "Calves, goats..."

"And don't forget the chickens!" I laughed, as I hopscotched after her.

Nana picked up my laugh and made it louder.

"Aren't they ridiculous sometimes?" Nana replied, stopping between two poles and hopping around on one leg as she imitated a rooster she called Canturrón who was always dancing around a hen while it dragged wing against the ground.

"You need to twist your head and stare at the ground, too, Nana, if you are going to act like that stupid rooster. Like this, look."

Crooking my neck like the flame-red rooster and tucking my head tight against my shoulder, I circled round and round and crowed brainless.

"You and I have been living with chickens too long," Nana said, still laughing. "Come, I have something to show you."

Without opening any doors, we walked through the walls of several half-fallen sheds until we came to a small clearing surrounded by clumps of dead and dying bushes. There Nana came to a stop and pointed to a large patch of barren ground. Scattered throughout were several scabs of bark and kindling.

The Grandfather Fires

"This used to be the woodlot."

Falling to her knees, Nana dug both hands into the old kindling and tossed handfuls of bark into the air.

"If we keep still enough and listen closely," she said, in the shower of splinters, "even as this ancient sawdust falls through space, I am sure we can find some poetry here. A father maybe, telling his son that here he chopped wood as a small boy. And his father before him, too, and his father before him on down the line like many mirrors."

"Maybe they even used the same ax," I suggested.

"Oh, that's when it's best, when oldie things are kept safe snug and used by younger people," Nana agreed, looking up at me. "I still have one of my great-grandmother needles. There was a time when I used it on every patch, but now I seldom do for fear of wearing away the point. Young girls and old grandmother needles! Old grandfather axes and little boys! Now, that's poetry!"

Nana pushed her hand under the carpet of kindling, swam it through the bark, and brought it up with a handful of sawdust and moist earth.

"And when the boy, who I think would be just about your age, believes in the grandfather ax, nothing can stop him from putting his own handle to the iron head. He falls on one knee right before he chops, dips his hand far into the old wood like this, and feels."

Nana pushed her hand wrist-deep into the sea of sticks.

"I can just hear him saying, 'I feel a little heat down there, like the ashes of...'"

"Old campfires," I interrupted.

"Exactly! The grandfather fires!"

Nana paused for a moment, her hand quiet under the bark. Then, with her hand exploding upward in a storm of splinters, she exclaimed, "Fire! Fire! I love fire!"

Startled, I jumped back as she burst into laughter.

"Fire is an old woman's best friend," she explained, still laughing. "She is better prepared to meet whatever might come her way with a few flames, than if she props herself up like a silly, a cane in one hand, an umbrella in the other."

She dug both hands into the kindling pile and showered another handful of splinters all around us.

"Let me ask you a question," she said, looking at the sawdust sticking to her hands, and clapping them clean. "Have you ever noticed how old people walk like little bent birds, while little children sometimes imitate old people by strutting around like big birds?"

"Yes."

"Can that be poetry?"

"It could be, I guess. Sometimes animals and people look a little alike and do many of the same things."

"Maybe it's because that's what they are."

Cooling an Angry Angel

"Can this be poetry?" Nana asked, still on her knees and slapping her hands free of the last splinter. "An ugly blacksmith wrapped in muscle called Slop Mouth."

I laughed as she slathered her tongue around the blacksmith.

"Don't laugh, it's a serious question. One day he reaches into his scrap heap and picks up his last ingot."

"What's a ingot?"

"An ingot? An ingot is a big chunk of raw iron. Sometimes people call it pig. Reaching for the last of his wood, the grime-encrusted smith finds it moldy and unusable against the ground."

"Because it's wet?"

"Yes. He slips immediately into anger, tosses it aside, and goes into his usual grumble of smolder. Pig-headed that he is, he begins to pound the metal cold. Bathed in sweat and cursing the wood with each blow, he keeps tusking away at the cold slab with his sledge until he makes it glow. Sparks fly. Finally, he tosses the angry tin into a trough to cool, and rests his hammer quiet across the anvil."

"What was he making?"

"Wait a minute. Free of smoke now, his mouth lies still. Reaching into the water, he pulls out his metal. He has pounded it from pig and into an angel with lace-thin wings, a weather-vane. Climbing to the top of his forge, he anchors it there. A breeze comes, and the angel turns from one direction to another. Can that be poetry?"

I thought for a moment, then replied, "Yes, that's poetry."

"What's poetry? The angel now or the pig that used to be?"

"The turning."

"Yes," Nana replied, "the turning."

The Precious Bone

Still kneeling on the rotten wood, Nana looked up at me and inquired further. "What about this, can this be poetry? An enormous, mud-slopped and crusty elephant."

"No, not that," I said firmly, standing tall and looking down on her. "An elephant can't be poetry. Too ugly."

"Well, for some people maybe not the elephant itself because they consider themselves above the poor animal. Too clean for his crusty ways, maybe?"

Nana winked at me.

"But how about how sleep comes gentle to its tired eye so ringed with wrinkles? You know how clubfooted they are, how they plod heavy, looking always down because their trunks pull their faces to the very ground. And yet, they love those trunks, I'm sure, because that is all the mouth they have."

"We studied elephants in Mrs. Tandemschnocker's class, but she called them packy derms. Probably because they can carry heavy loads. I'm sure it's true."

Nana studied me in silence for a long moment, then said, "We've all seen elephants at school, those poor children of God. Wandering behind their leaders with their eyes closed they go, from water hole to water hole in long lines through the vast savannah."

"I don't know what savanna means? Mrs. Tandemschnocker hasn't taught us."

"I think savannah means a waste place in somewhere they call Africa. The poor things just follow, wordless. Elephants remind me of lines where people lead themselves. Tail to trunk they lumber. At times the leader, who is usually a female, carries with it and fondles a fallen tusk like a lesson she wants to pass on. She tastes the dead bone. She passes it to the one behind him. From trunk to trunk, never dropping it, nurturing the piece of ivory so, kissing it, actually, back and forth among them. Elephants and us are almost the same thing, you know, especially when it comes to things we don't want to forget."

"That's what Mrs. Tandemschnocker told us. That we were just like elephants."

Nana studied me in silence again, then she said, "You are. In the memories we are. They say elephants never forget. Day by day we also grow, but there are memories that make time stand still."

"How?"

"Because they are so precious. Like the elephants carrying the tusk of their dead brother, we won't put those flashes in the mind away for one lone moment, even when we go to bed."

Nana fell silent for a moment, then started up again.

"I saw an elephant close up once. It didn't see me watching. Even now, I still remember how gentle is the mercy God has for shutting the eye of his driest, most clubfooted creature. Do you think that could be poetry?"

"I suppose that kind of elephant could be poetry."

"I agree."

"Maybe I can write a poem about an elephant for Mrs. Tandemschnocker, Nana."

"That would make a good pome. With little ones following."

The Little Man

"Follow me."

Without getting up, Nana crawled on her hands and knees back and forth over the woodlot.

"What are you looking for, Nana?" I asked, walking behind her as she dragged herself over a long, splintered pole while holding the faded roses safely out of her knee's path.

"A moment, just a moment. I'll find it here in time."

She criss-crossed the woodlot pushing aside the larger chunks of wood and turning over the smaller barks. Finally, she lifted an old board and brushed aside the sawdust underneath until she exposed the earth.

"Here, come here. Kneel down," she said, patting the splinters.

I knelt beside her on the rotten wood. My eyes followed her pointing finger to the spot she had swept clean.

"I don't see anything."

"That's right. We have to wait. You can't make poetry happen. It comes to you. It's like an apple. Nobody can make an apple happen. You have to wait with your eye on the branch and watch because the water is slow in the trunk. Trunk water is what actually makes the blossom apple out in the end. The sun and wind add the color. Mostly the sun. Here, get closer to the ground, like this, and be quiet."

Nana put her elbows to the ground and rested her head on both hands a few inches above the rotten wood.

I felt the wood splinters chipping into my knees, but I obeyed. I put my elbows on the barks, lowered my head and propped it between my hands. Nana lowered her head another inch closer to the splinters and motioned me to do the same.

My face skimmed the splinters. I smelled damp rot.

"Nana, do you know what you're..."

"Quiet, don't move!"

"Nana, there is nothing there!"

Nana ignored me as she kept staring at the ground. Suddenly, she shouted out.

"Yes, there is! Look!"

She pointed to a little black speck in the clearing that struggled with a white dot between its pinchers. The little black shadow pulled and pushed on the crumb trying to get it past a tiny pebble. Sand shot out in six different directions around the animal's feet.

"It's only an ant, Nana!" I said, annoyed that all I got out of ten thousand splinters on my knees was a little black nothing.

"Watch," Nana said, ignoring my disgust, her eye glued to the earth. "It's appling out in its own way."

Though the ground gave way time and again around the ant, it never released its precious load. Finally, it managed to push the food crumb up, over, and past the giant grain.

"Apple!" Nana shouted, excitedly. "Now, that's poetry! Listen to the silence around the little black man!"

She pushed herself to her knees and started clapping.

"Cheers! Cheers! I hear his song! I sing it along with him! 'No one sees me! No one hears me! No one knows but me!'"

Putting her arm around me, she placed her finger almost on the animal's back and continued. "That's poetry speaking. Do you see how very long we have to wait for poetry? The little man has to wait even longer than the ant between his victories. And sometimes ants go unnoticed because they are so small and so close to the ground. But when their glory happens, it too pushes up and makes a ripple on the other side, on God's side of the sky, because ants also are important in the blue."

Nana placed her finger before the ant and cleared a path in the splinters ahead of it.

"That's poetry! That's poetry! Hard work. Nothing like making pomes!"

The ant continued from splinter point to splinter point until it disappeared.

"Yep. You can't make jelly until you shake the tree."

Nana looked at me to see if I would ask what she meant, but I remained silent.

"That's just something of a memory I have of what people used to say back then. Jelly is hard work."

High Poetry

"Nana, do you have a lot of memories about the long ago?"

"About the long ago? Oh, I carry with me things like this scar that I still remember," she said, rising from the broken wood and pointing to the shiny stripe on her arm. "But what I have lost is probably what I hold closest. Sounds hard to understand, don't it?"

"A little, but I still want you to tell me them. The memories, I mean."

Rising up behind her, I brushed the kindling off my knees and pulled several splinters from my elbows.

"I like to call those memories and thoughts, 'high poetry.'"

"High poetry?"

"Yes, high poetry is the feeling in your heart when God, after He has answered every prayer, on His very own and without you even asking, answers thoughts you've kept hidden deep wrapped in desire. You'll understand someday, when you are finished growing."

Nana looked at me for a minute without saying anything, then she continued.

"All his life the poor man leaves these thoughts unsaid because he believes himself very little among the important things God has to busy Himself with. He knows that what he's longing for cannot possibly come his way. Why should he take up God's time asking for what isn't there? After all, by the time a person grows up, God usually has already given him all he has asked for."

Nana looked at me again, then continued.

"But, that's where high poetry comes in, when God laughs his little laugh at us because we think He can't hear secret thoughts we roll around inside our thinking."

"But God isn't laughing at us, right?" I asked.

"That's correct. God never laughs at us, only at our paintings. Can you imagine God not being able to hear what we think, or better yet, can you imagine Him not being able to laugh? Remember the angel painter?"

"Yes."

"Oh, I tell you! God laughing is a sound that graces an ear more beautifuler than the most sparklie earring!" Nana exclaimed. "I have always believed that."

I remembered the earrings.

I reached into my pocket.

The salt was warm.

The Light in the Stone

"Nana, what is your most important memory?"

Nana reached down and picked up three small stones.

"For a long time, I have had one memory and two secret thoughts. The thoughts, I have never spoken to anyone, not even to God. They are too precious. But I'm going to share them with you."

She rubbed the dirt off the dull gray rocks. Spitting on the one with the most stubborn dirt, she rubbed it clean.

"Did you see when I picked up these little stones? Has it crossed your mind they have seen everyone who has passed by here, but no one has seen them except for you and me now?"

"I bet somebody sometime saw at least one of the them once," I argued.

"Fine, perhaps you are right. In fact, I'm sure you are right." She placed her hand on my shoulder.

"But what about the light in the stone?"

"The light in the stone?"

"Yes. Close your eyes."

I closed them. Immediately, I heard a loud crack as she banged the stones together.

"Keep your eyes closed. I am going to show you something no one has ever seen before."

In the dark, I heard several more cracks.

"There," she said, finally. "Now, open your eyes."

I opened them and looked at the pieces which Nana was holding before me. The sun was inside the stones. The gray rocks were gray no longer. Inside, one stone was very black, the other a dark green, and, to my surprise, the last was no longer a winter-wren drab, but white with tiny, red streaks running everywhere. All three stones were loaded with crystals that changed colors as the sun broke light from one glass flake to another.

"You are the first to see these crystals," Nana said, simply. "I am talking from the beginning of the world. That's the way it is on the outside, gray. But can anybody tell what goes around and around inside the heart?"

Nana paused for me to answer.

"No."

"You are right, again. The stone has to be broken. It's the only way to see how the sun shines inside. What I'm going to share with you about me is what goes around and around."

"Now?"

"No. When we reach the top of the hill. Here," she said, handing me the stone full of tiny red veins and tossing the other two back into the dark rubble of the old wood lot.

The Mysterious Matrix

"Have you ever noticed the night with its stars?" Nana asked.

"Of course. Every one has seen the stars."

"That's not what I asked. I asked, 'Have you ever noticed the night with its stars?'"

"Of course, the stars are plain to see. I'm sure I've even seen some planets, too. Did you know they are bigger than we are, Nana?"

"Is that right?"

"Yes, we learned that last year. What you need to remember about planets," I instructed, "is that they are the ones that go around and around in a milky way. If you want, some night we can come out and try to find some. I can teach you the planets, but you have to do it at night. Mrs. Tandemschnocker said that's the only time they come out. During the day the sun is bigger than at night and it hides them in the light. The main thing to remember about planets is that they are still there even if you can't see them."

"That's poetry, when you know its there but you can't see it. Maybe tonight after this climb you can take me around to find the planets. I find the night itself very interesting, that darkness between the stars."

"Do you think the night could be poetry, too, Nana?"

"Oh, absolutely! Night is not just nothing, you know. It's God's mysterious glue—a poet would call it matrix—the mysterious matrix in the sky which holds the planets and stars together and apart at the same time."

"Can God can do anything He wants to with His May tricks?"

"Anything. Turn salt into sugar, even."

The Talking Conch

"I know you've never seen the sea,..."

"I have too seen it, Nana, on Mrs. Tandemschnocker's world. She keeps it on one corner of her desk in a box so it won't roll off and she don't let anybody even touch that corner. Each country is a different color, and the ocean is blue."

"Yes it is, and it has its gentle poetry, too. Do you want me to tell you how?"

"Yes, but don't talk about the different countries. The names Mrs. Tandemschnocker calls them aren't even real words."

"Alright. If I say something that isn't a real word, stop me and I'll explain."

"I will."

"And now, the sea. I saw it when I was a little girl. I remember the grownups were talking about the war. I don't know which war. When I heard them there on the shore talking of all the battles and pointing out, the waves were so loud they drowned me out because they kept breaking forever. The water was heavy. I thought I was dead because I was so small. Immensely."

"Stop! Is that a real word?"

"Yes. Immensely means two different things at once. Being very, very big and being very, very small."

"That's confusing."

"That's the sea. There are many words like that, too, and when you think on them, all you do is bump back and forth between them. Anyway, as I was standing on the beach, I looked far out across the water to where they were pointing, to where they said the war was. I don't know if it was the war I couldn't see or the ocean that wouldn't let me, but I thought to myself, 'Something this immense cannot possibly have any idea I'm standing here.'"

"Is the ocean really blue, Nana?"

"Yes, many different blues. Some blues are so blue they're green.

But as I was saying, standing on that shore, I found out that the great ocean can be gentle. As I stood on the shore, I noticed a young woman. She was crying. I could tell she had been crying for a long time, she was black. Then it happened. The sea in its enormousnessness..."

"Stop...!"

"... Yes, that's a real word. It means a very heavy kind of big— the enormousnessness in the sea noticed that girl. It reached deep into its heart of water, and in its own form of kindness—you understand that word—it brought up a huge shell and laid it gently on the sand at her feet."

"Was it empty?"

"There wasn't an animal living in it, but it wasn't empty. There it was on the sand, the shell, a pink curl turning white, like an offering. An offering is when you give to get peace. She reached down and picked it up. Pale and pink, like a good, warm heart, it was, that shell so big, in the palm of that black girl."

Nana paused, remembering.

"Oh! What beautiful colors, white and black connected by human pink! Anyway, she held the conch to her ear, then pushed it away and looked at it as if there were something inside. She put it back to her ear and listened to it for a long time. Then—and I will always remember this—with the shell still to her ear, and as if there was someone she recognized inside the shell guiding her, she looked out to sea. She looked about the waves back and forth listening to the shell until she fixed her eyes on something."

"What was it?"

"Well, I looked too, but I couldn't see anything. Maybe it was because I didn't know what she was crying about. Still listening to the shell and her eye on the sea, she stopped crying. Actually, I thought I saw her smile, but I don't know. It could have been just the sea turning on its side or the sun splashing off the water to her face. Anyway, she stared at the spot in the sea almost as if she was talking to it. Then, she smiled, as if saying goodbye. She turned around and walked away with the shell still telephoning in her ear. I went back several times, but I never saw her come to the shore again. Later, they told me she had lost her sailor. She reminded me of Doña Arna. You know, the one who lives five farms down from us."

"The one everybody calls crazy?"

"Yes. She, too, lost her love to the water."

"Do you think I will ever see the ocean, Nana, so I can write poetry on it?"

65

"Yes. You will. Everyone does at some time or another, but you don't have to go to the ocean to see it. Sometimes the sea comes to you."

Pale to Nothing

"We are in poetry right now, did you know that? Look around you. What do you see?" Nana asked.

"Nothing, just that old rosebush."

I pointed to a tangled shrub that had turned thorny during many years of living alone in the Old Place. The few leaves it would have during the summer were far behind in green for this time of spring. There was not enough water living in the dry wood.

"What else do you see on that old rosebush?"

"It's not going to have any roses, that's for sure."

"Let's walk alongside it and take a closer look."

Nana pulled me with her. We walked along the tangle slowly while keeping our eyes on the old shrub.

"Now what do you see as we walk along the brambles of the winter hedge?"

I was going to tell her about our shadows on the sticks, but she interrupted.

"Look at us, how we walk in shadow. Can you see how we ghost along, sieving ourselves from branch to branch and the thorns cut?"

"Is sieving a real word?"

"Yes. It's everything passing from big to very little then pales to nothing."

"Is it the same as sifting, like flour?"

"Yes, when you unbone and not let even skin pass through, keeping only what is sweet, the fruit."

"What does 'pales to nothing' mean?"

"Pale to nothing?" Nana took a deep breath. "That's hard even for me to understand. You see, so many things come from mist and go to mist. The best I can explain it is walking on a trail in a forest. There you meet so many people who appear in a bend from nowhere. They look at you, pass beside you in silence and keep going. You move ahead looking behind for one last look at them, to see where they went, but they are gone. That's what 'pale to nothing' means, I think. But I don't know."

Nana caught me staring at her, studying her, as I tried to understand what she meant.

"You're looking at me," she said, accusingly, "as if I knew the meaning of the word 'means.' I don't know what 'mean' means."

I remained locked in silence.

"You don't understand, do you? I don't understand myself either," she offered, "and that's why when I think about it, I don't think about it for very long."

There was a speck of sadness in her voice.

The Braver Blood

"But you know what?" she said, with new spring in her voice. "Joy that comes after sadness is wonderful poetry because it points to life. The red, red tulips!"

Nana jumped up slightly on 'tulips,' and her voice followed.

"In spring," she continued, excitedly, "those beautiful bulbies are the first to break ground and offer up that first fistful of blood that starts the colors of summer running again! And those dandelions in the meadow. How they follow! A little runty because of the lingering cold perhaps, but they can't wait, either. Being braver than the other blooms, they risk their yellow in those low March winds, but they hold on to it to become the gold that in the end dapples the meadow's back."

She poked her finger into my side.

"And you thought they were only pesky weeds!" she exclaimed, laughing.

"You are the one who calls them pesky weeds, Nana! I've seen you attacking them with your hoe!"

She tickled me again. I pushed my right hand toward her right side pretending I was going to tickle her there, but at the last moment, I tried one of God's May tricks and curved my right hand to the left and pushed it like lightning into her left side. The two of us laughed and tickled long. As I poked tickles into her wherever I could, I noticed how tender she was. Sanctuary, the word she had shown me, came to mind.

"We best get on with this climb if we ever expect to see more poetry," she said. "Come, I have something else to show you. Poetry can be quite simple, too. I saw it just three bends up the road the other day when I was out here gathering the goats."

Nana led the way back to the road. Grasping the string of her apron, she lifted it slightly out of snagging danger and skipped lightly over the scattered poles. She looked like a queen holding her robe up from the mud while crossing a puddle. As we walked beside the chimney stack and under the burnt crow, I ran out in front of her and led the way over the waves of the garden ground. I stepped over the barbed fence, and she followed.

"Oops!"

I stopped and looked back.

There was Nana, snagged.

She tugged twice on the apron, but the barb held. She gave a stronger yank and the apron came loose, leaving a large patch on the fence. She examined the torn apron for a moment, then released the cloth.

"Oh, well," she said, with little concern as she tightened what remained of the apron around her waist and patted its upper part, "there's still plenty of apron left up here. Besides, this old pile of sticks could sure use a rose."

The Two Philosophers

Once on the road, Nana fell into a brisk pace. We rounded a curve in the road, and she stopped.

"There. See those two children? That's what I wanted to show you."

Under a tree, grassy except where a low swing had peeled away a strip of grass down to dirt, a small girl and her younger brother played while their mother swayed slowly back and forth.

"She is too old to be swinging on that baby swing," I said. "Look at her legs. Her knees are dragging ground."

"Yes. I am glad you noticed that, because I hadn't. Skinned knees and children go together. Sometimes on the mother, sometimes on them. But what I wanted to show you were the two little ones. Notice how they look almost like philosophers?"

"What are philosophers?"

"Philosophers means when there is only one pile of sand and two people share it."

I studied the two children as they played. After each exchange of grains, they would burst out in laughter. Regardless of how much sand they started out with and offered each other, both ended up with nothing.

"They start out with sand and end up with laughter," I said.

"You know, I hadn't seen that, but you're right."

"Watch how she looks after them while they play," I instructed Nana.

As the mother swayed gently in the air beside the playing children, she reached out her hand and touched the children on the head. She swung past the younger child, and brushed the girl's black curls. On the backward swing, she reached out for the boy, ran her hand through his hair and floated on.

"You're right, again," said Nana. "Her heart is so happy! I can see it glowing with the glaze of fifty candles on a cake! I know, I know!"

Nana was so excited, her face beamed.

"She is feeling the bud, the flower, and the fruit all at once! I know! I know! I'm a mother! Maybe we could create a word for it!" she exclaimed, turning to me.

"Create a word for what?"

"The feeling! For the feeling! That's what poetry is, feeling! Feeling you can see and hear!"

In her excitement, the words stumbled over each other.

She puckered her lips and rolled them round as if tasting some delicious fruit.

"I've got it! I've got it!" she yelled out, suddenly.

She dropped to her knees, placed one hand on either side of my face and squeezed my cheeks inward until my lips fished out an inch past my nose.

"Budflowerfruit! That's it! Say it! Say it!"

"Bud flower fruit," I managed to puff out through her squeezing hands. "What's bud flower fruit?"

"That's it! Yes! Yes! No! No! It isn't! You have to say it all at once!" she cried out, as she squeezed my cheeks even tighter. Between her hands, I could see my face paper thin.

I attempted the words several times, but they felt strange. My tongue thickened up before I was halfway through the sounds. I tried again, but my lips got in the way.

"Nana, I can't say anything when you are pushing my face together!" I sputtered.

Nana released me.

I could speak the words.

My mouth was free.

"Bud flower fruit."

"No, you are saying it wrong. It's budflowerfruit."

"Budflower fruit? What's budflower fruit?"

"No. You're still saying it wrong. It's budflowerfruit!"

"Budflowerfruit? Nana, my tongue doesn't know how to say that. Is that a real word?"

"Yes! It's a real word and you said it! You said it! That's poetry! Seeing what isn't there and talking about it makes it be there! Words make life. Now, say it! After me!"

Nana tightened her lips together and puckered them again into the same knot she had made before. She grasped my hands in hers, and together we brought forth the word.

"Budflower...," she began... "...fruit!" I ended.

"I did it!...   ...You did it!" she echoed.

"Budflowerfruit," we shouted together.

"You talked poetry! How did it feel?" she asked, excitedly. She then answered her own question with yet another question.

"Juicy?"

Laughter broke from her mouth and her wrinkles spread it all over her face.

"Wet and spitty! That's how it felt, Nana."

"That's poetry!"

Together we tossed the new word between us several times, laughing. Nana spit on me, and I spit on Nana, but neither of us minded. As Nana laughed, I could see her two missing teeth. In the laughter of the budflowerfruit, the longest laughter on the hill, the tiny holes were barely there.

"Let's climb!" we shouted together.

The Top of the Hill

Our hands moved toward each other through the laughter of the budflowerfruit and found each other.

We wound our way upward following the turning ground as the road squeezed between tall boulders and among groves of trees. Several times I raced ahead of Nana and hid in the bend ahead. Once, I tossed a stone into the thicket across the road to distract her so I could jump on her from behind the tree where I was hiding to maytrick her. But while I watched for her to appear around the bend, she cut across the forest behind me, came back onto the road farther up, and maytricked me.

"Last one up the hill is going to be the last one to get there!" she called out.

I came out of my hiding place, walked up the road and found her sitting on a rock with her hands quietly folded on her apron.

"If you are still tired, we can rest a little longer," she offered.

"I'm not tired," I said, and, like a puppy outwitted by the simplest bunny, I sat down at her feet.

"It doesn't matter who gets where first," she said. "What counts is getting there before the door closes."

I couldn't think of anything to answer. Nana was just too wise for me.

"Rested?" she asked, after a few minutes.

"I'm ready if you are."

Nana rose from the boulder, gave me a hand, and we continued. As we climbed higher on the hill, the trees went from bushy to pointy. The air was fresher, and the clouds appeared closer. Several times, Nana stopped to rest.

"Songbirds here sing a different tune, have you noticed?"

"Yes. I have never seen these birds at home, though," I said, pointing to a blue-gray warbler twittering on a branch.

"Oh, as long as you can hear a bird sing, you're always home," Nana replied. "Ready?"

"Yes."

"It's time you led the climb," she announced. "I'll follow."

After climbing several bends, I waited for Nana to catch up.

"Are you birdlooking, Nana?" I shouted back, when she stopped for the fourth time.

"No bird," she replied, leaning against a dying tree, "but I'm high enough to hear a song, and that's just as good."

Twice I walked back down the hill and, though she didn't want me to take her hand, I helped her over several humps on the road.

I was tired, too, but I kept climbing. As we neared the top, the slope became much steeper.

"Don't give up, Nana, we're almost there! I can already see the smoke from town!" I shouted, as I looked up and saw the road humped against the sky.

"When you can see the smoke below, everything is almost over," she yelled back, breathing hard. "You must be very near the top!"

"I'm even with the clouds, Nana!"

"Wait for me there, don't lose ground. Don't bother coming down anymore. I'm going to make it because I am."

I scrambled the last few yards up the road and reached the peak.

Below me, Nana was holding up her apron, as though by holding it, she could lighten her load. She looked up and saw me standing on the peak.

"Just a few more steps, Nana!"

She grasped her apron tighter and lengthened her steps.

"Finally!" she said, breathless beside me.

"What's another word for 'top of the hill?'" she asked, releasing her apron and still panting.

"Oh, that's easy, Nana," I answered. "Crest."

From the crest, the two gravel tracks we had followed upward began to coast slowly down the other side. Side by side they curled around boulders and twisted through trees as they waved themselves farther and farther down the slopes. Faster and faster the two tracks unrolled themselves like twin ribbons of earth. Whenever the right one twisted itself to go around a thicket, the left one followed. When the left one angled off to miss a boulder, the right one went immediately beside it. In the distance, the two finally became one.

"See how the two come to a point down in the town, Nana?" I pointed.

"I was thinking the same thing," she replied. "They converge."

"Converge. That's a real word and I bet I know what that means.

Coming together, right?"

"Yes. Coming together."

Cenicero

Below us, buried in haze, lay Cenicero.

"What does Cenicero mean?" I asked as we stood on the hill looking down at the streets that stretched out in several directions from where the two gravel tracks had converged.

"Ash heap," Nana replied.

"What's the story of it?"

"My great grandfather's family was the first to come to this valley," Nana said, sweeping her hand over the green velvet cradled in the rolling hills. "They named the valley Verdistancia, and the little settlement they named Cenicero."

"What does Verdistancia mean?"

"Verdistancia can mean two things. One is green distance. Mame Timia, my grandmother, wasn't even born then. For a long time it stayed small, just a few homes over by that hill. Everybody used that low place where the town is now to throw away their ashes. Mame Timia told me that as people began moving in from other parts and the village grew, they started building down there."

She pointed through a light gray blanket of smoke that covered the town.

"The O'Childs and Flora's people moved in later. That's their place over by the river."

"Mr. O'child. Is he the one past the Old Place?" I asked.

"That's him. After Cesario Penitente, Mr. O'child is Grampo's toppest friend. And Flora. Well, you know Mrs. Switchfoot."

"I know her all over again every autumn at apple time," I sighed, thinking of our neighbor and Nana's best friend.

Nana laughed. "Not even a sister would sit as long as she does peeling apples with me."

"And drying," I added.

"I'm good at that," Nana said with a chuckle. "Been doing it up to now from the moment I was born. All grandmothers do."

"How old was your grandmother?"

"Mame Timia was almost a hundred when she died. She said she was the first child born in Cenicero."

"A hundred?" I said, in surprise. "Then she was old enough to know the whole story."

Nana laughed. "She knew the story of how stories began. She got all of her's from a dying king."

"Really?"

"Yes, in a bottle."

"In a bottle?"

"Yes. She told me that her mother's mother told her there was a king once who knew all the stories in the world. One day, he fell very sick, and his magicians, knowing they wouldn't hear his stories any more, got a bottle and rushed to his bedside. 'Talk into the bottle! Talk into the bottle!' they cried. And they hurried him, and he did. All night. And then he died. And when Mame Timia's grandfather moved here, they brought the bottle with them. And because Mame Timia was the first child and there were no other children to play with, her mother just opened up the bottle for her whenever she wanted someone to play with."

"I don't believe that," I said, shaking my head.

"It does sound farfetched, doesn't it?"

"For sure," I said.

"Well, it really is farfetched, if you think about it, because Mexico is far away. That's where they came from. And Spain is even farther across the sea. For me it's true though, because I've heard of important message bottles going around the world just by floating on the ocean. And the people were saved by the message."

Nana pointed to Cenicero. "There are a lot of stories down there."

The square head of the tallest building poked up through the gray haze. It was the bank. Beside it, two other buildings which I recognized as the shoe store and the meat market were stacked on top of each other. The shoes were on top of the meat.

"Is that where Mrs. Tandemschnocker is building her new house?" Nana asked, pointing to a bulge of new growth that protruded out from the main body.

"Yes."

"I can see the cranes picking up the pieces, wall chunks. Can you?"

"Yes. Feels a little smokey, doesn't it?" I asked.

"Smokey? What do you mean?" she asked.

"I mean the town is sad all over. Like under a curtain," I answered, pointing to the gray.

"Perhaps the smokey is trying to tell us something?"

"Like what?" I asked.

"Well, I was thinking that maybe we could take that sad smokey..."

"...and turn it into a poetry?" I interrupted.

"Yes," Nana chuckled. "We can turn it into a poetry. Poetry is finding out. What do you think that sad smokey is trying to tell us?"

"Maybe too many trees under the gray, and that they won't be able to have enough leaves."

Mrs. Tandemschnocker came to mind. I felt a little sad for her.

"She really isn't as bad as they say, you know, Nana."

"Who?"

"Mrs. Tandemschnocker."

"Oh, I agree. Nobody is. But sometimes it takes a lump or two in the bitter black to make us see things a little differently. You are thinking about the pomes you have to write for her, aren't you?"

"Yes."

"Well, maybe you are wondering what I sometimes wonder in my own sad smokey."

"What's that?"

"I often think the world is quite full of poetry, but sometimes we build pomes like row houses to put it in."

Reaching down, Nana placed her hand under my chin and cradled my face upward as she did the ripe peaches when she separated them from the tree.

"You will do just fine with whatever you want to turn into a poetry for Mrs. Tandemschnocker," she replied. "I know you can turn anything you want into a poetry. And you know how I know?"

"How?"

"Because you've already taught me the planets."

Nana gazed at me for a moment, then, turning around, she stood looking back.

"I see my house," she said. "All of Verdistancia."

She pointed to our neighbor who was still in his orchard under the grapevine.

"There's Mano Tiberio and his long dog Cejano."

"He's always slinking behind him everywhere he goes like a pet weasel."

"I know. You remember that grapevine he was pruning when we

went by this morning?"

"Yes. He's always cutting on it."

"That grapevine belonged to his father. They called him the rusty angel of Cenicero. Someday I'll tell you the story about that tin angel weather vane on top of his appleshed, and how they say his grandfather carried the little grape slip in his mouth all the way from Mexico to here."

"Why?"

"To keep it alive when he was crossing the desert. And way over there next to Mano Tiberio's orchard is Don Zenaido's house. Can you see it?"

"Yes. Is he the blind one?" I asked.

"Yes. And over there by that cliff where the river curves into the mountain, that's where Don Macías lives. Can you see the little wood shed to the side?"

"Barely."

"That's where he does all his carving."

"He sure can carve that wood. I wouldn't be surprised if he isn't turning those cottonwood roots we saw him carrying this morning into santos."

"What are santos?"

"Wood carvings. Saints. People or animals."

When the Cherry Shined

Nana pointed out several more houses buried in the haze of Verdistancia.

"Most of them are pretty old," she said, wiping her forehead with one arm and drying it on the sleeve of the other. "They all go back a long, long time."

She dried her arm and, as she rolled down her sleeve, I saw the scar.

"Nana, your scar, remember? You promised to tell me when we reached the top of the hill. And you also promised to tell me your closest memory, and your two secret thoughts, too."

Nana was quiet for a few moments. Then she looked up and searched the sky as when she looked around and around under her apple trees to make sure she had picked every bit of fruit. Gathering her thoughts, she asked, "Do you remember the mother in the swing?"

"The philosopher mother?"

"Yes. Well, mothers are poetry, too, when they become lonely because their children grow up into men and leave. They begin to live in expectation."

"Does expectation mean like when you are waiting for something to happen?" I asked.

"Yes, waiting for something to come. Expectation is mothers in the morning preparing their house for the daily things, like dusting shelves and picking lint carefully out of forgotten corners. They push the feathers through the portraits without toppling a single frame and bring out a spearful of lint on every straw. And they do it all without even looking, because all the while they are somewhere else."

"What do you mean?"

"They are searching for their children who have turned into men, and their minds are far away. From the trophy shelf they go and stand in the doorway. They reach for the doormat without taking their eyes off the horizon. They shake it and shake it as they search for their children in the dust of their mind. But the children do not appear."

She paused, looked at me, then continued.

"All day long among their house things they spend nurturing the strangest of desires."

"What is that?" I interrupted.

"To return that evening to that doorway and find a mat soiled with tracks and made beautiful with mud. But they find the mat clean. The moon rises, and they realize it's night. They give the mat one more shake, find it disappointingly dustless and turn their thoughts to bed. They fall asleep, still praying for dust they can call familiar."

"But, what about those who don't have children?"

"They have to get up in the morning, too. Everybody has to rise in the end."

Nana paused for a moment, then continued.

"Many times I ask myself, who does a childless woman get up for in the morning? What could she find so valuable and precious on earth worth getting up for if it ain't a boy or a girl?"

Nana stopped and looked at me again.

"I remember when all my children were young. I always fell asleep thinking of them, and in the morning they were still on my mind. Not once did I ever put any of them down in the dark."

"You know, Nana, I would have liked the old days. What was it like back then, in the olden time?"

"In the olden time? Well, in that long ago everyone had to work long hours doing whatever, even the children. In those days you didn't need school to know things. Everybody naturally understood what was good and important. Like when the apple was ripe, or what it meant when the cherry shined."

"When the cherry shined?"

"Yes. How the sun fell on the cherry told you how long it still had to stay on the wood to suck itself sugary from the tree. Even little children knew that. They knew everything without going to school. Like how to pack fruit in sawdust to keep the September juices gathered crisp all the way to April. Or how much water to keep adding to the bucket in the fruithouse so the apples could drink whenever they wanted all winter long to keep their wet juices red."

Nana fell silent for a moment.

"Work," she said, after gathering her thoughts, "there was a lot of work. Work was our school. As for the scar, it happened during apple time. As you know, there is always one apple that grows the highest on every tree where the sun washes it golden, the most delicious one, you know, and...."

"....and you went after it and fell, right?"

"But it healed," Nana said, laughing.

Kissing the Bone

"Now tell me the memory."

Nana's face tightened a little.

"The memory? That has been a cold that just won't warm up or go away. Remember by the river how I told you there are some diseases for which there is no remedy in the meadow? Well, I have carried that cold memory forever like..."

"...like the elephant and the bone?"

Nana put her arm around me and pulled me close. The rough denim pocket she had sewn over the faded roses of her apron rubbed my face.

"Yes, like the elephant and the precious bone. I have kissed it back and forth in my mind forever to keep it alive."

"What's the memory?

"My memory?"

"Yes."

She waited, and I thought maybe she had changed her mind. "Yes. The memory. Tell me it. I want to know."

"My memory is your mother. Since she left, there has been no lack of lonesome."

"Like an ailment of a hundred years?" I asked, remembering the word she had told me at the bottom of the hill when we had started climbing.

"A hundred going on ten thousand years, seems like," Nana said, pulling me tighter into herself.

Tucked tight against Nana's side, I felt as though there was an opening under her arm where I had tickled her, and she had put me in it. I fit the hole with no space left over.

"Influenza, flu. You were so tiny, days old, then," she continued. "It hit so many families. Everybody lost somebody. We tried every remedy we knew. We raked the hillsides for oshá until we hit the rock layer, combed the meadows for it until the ground was bare. And the wonderful Indian medicine helped with all its might, but she still fell sick hard. Your aunts all wanted to take you, but she would have none of it. 'I will not allow it! I will not allow it!' She kept saying that from her bed for two months."

I could feel Nana's grip on me tightening.

"Then, as she got weaker, it was, 'He will go with Nana. I will not have anyone else raise him. He will go with Nana.' Those were her words for about two weeks. In the end, drops of blood came up with her words, but she kept on whispering, 'Nana will name him, Nana will name him.'"

Nana placed both hands on my back and held me the tightest on the hill. "And I did name you. Eres mío, mi hijito. You are mine, my love. That is why I named you Mío. 'Mío' means mine in Spanish."

Nana spoke Spanish only when it was very important. Among her friends, to the grasshoppers when they were the thickest and were sucking up entire plants, as she put it, and to God. With God she always talked in loud Spanish.

"Eres mío, mi hijito," she repeated, as she patted my back gently. Under Nana's hand, I understood for the first time what my name meant. Mío meant I belonged.

"Nana, I feel like a baby elephant under the huge mother," I said, tight against her side.

"What do you mean?" she asked.

"Immense, remember? That's a real word, Nana. It means small but very big, like you did by the sea. The elephants, they all look so much alike. They are actually both one, like two drops, a big one and a little one, the mother and the baby."

"Yes, they are. And so are people. And it would not have been any different if you had been a girl. I would have named you Mía. It still means mine."

Still under Nana's arm, I looked up at Grandma. I imagined how beautiful my mother must have been. She had to have looked at least a little bit like Nana, her eyes perhaps, her nose, maybe even the tickles and the hole between her arm and heart.

"Nana, did my mother talk like you?"

"Oh, the two of us talked as you said, like two elephants, a big one and a little one, trunk to trunk, always kissing."

"Nana, what does your name mean?"

Nana smiled the most secret smile.

"What does my name mean?" she repeated. "You have never heard my name. My name is not 'Nana.'"

"It isn't?"

"No," she answered, through her smile, "my name is Altagracia. Alta means 'high' in Spanish. What do you think gracia means?"

"Grace?" I guessed.

Nana nodded and smiled wider. "Yes. Not very many boys your age could have known that, unless they had studied it in a book. And even then."

"High grace! Your name means 'high grace!'" I exclaimed.

"But your mother used to call me 'nana' when she was a little girl. Before she died, she left instructions that, growing up, you should call me 'nana,' too.

"And I have been calling you Nana."

"No. You have been calling me 'Nana.' I said 'nana.' 'Nana' and 'nana' are not the same. They are two different words. Listen to the pronounce. There is a big difference."

Carefully, she pronounced each word.

"'Nana,' and 'nana.' 'Nana' is English. 'Nana' is Spanish. Say them."

I imitated the sounds as closely as I had heard them.

"Nana. Nana. The words are different!" I exclaimed.

"'Nana' is what children say in Spanish when they are barely learning to call for their mothers. Say it again. 'Nana,'" Altagracia commanded.

"Nana, nana, nana," I repeated, being careful to sound as Spanish as I could.

"That's wonderful!" Nana exclaimed. "'Nana' is what you would have called Risa growing up."

"Risa," I repeated. "What does it mean?"

"Laughter."

"You mean my mother was laughter?"

"That she was."

"Risa. Risa."

I called my mother twice, wrapping my tongue around the sounds. Her name felt wonderful inside my mouth. It went deep all by itself.

Nana looked at me and said, "Mío, this minute, I have found out God has given me all I have asked for. You can call me Altagracia from now on if you want to because I love that name."

Zarcillos

"Nana? I mean, Altagracia."

"Yes?"

"How do you say 'I am' in Spanish?"

"Soy."

"How do you say 'I know?'"

"Sé. 'I don't know' is 'no sé.'"

"How do you say 'grandmother?'"

"'Abuela.' Sometimes we say 'Grama,' too, or 'Granma,' or 'Gramita.'"

"And how do you say 'you?'"

"It can be said three ways. You can say 'tú' if you are talking to someone you love very much like your dog or God. You say 'usted' if it's someone you respect very much like Benito Juárez. And if you should ever meet up with a queen like I did on the telephone, you would use 'su majestad,' which means 'your majesty.'"

"Who is Benito Juárez?"

"Don Benito was a freedom man for the people. A true Indian, like Abraham Lincoln, only Don Benito did it in Spanish."

"I know about Abraham Lincoln, Mrs. Tandemschnocker told us about him, and you're right, he was a freedom man."

"Yes."

"What does 'don' mean?"

"'Don' means a very respected person. It means 'sir,' which is more than many, many English 'misters' put together. And a very respected lady would be 'doña.' Do you remember the queen I saw on the telephone?"

"Yes."

"She was a 'doña.' 'Doña Gabriela,' everyone called her."

"Because she was a queen?"

"Oh, no," Altagracia replied, laughing, "she was far from queen. She was a curandera."

"What's a curandera?"

"A curandera is a people healer, someone who has been through many sicknesses and knows every remedy. There's not an illness whose face she has not seen."

"You knew all the names of the Indian remedies under the treehouse, are you a 'doña?'"

"Well, what do you think?"

"You know all the remedies."

"And you know Abraham Lincoln well enough to know he is a freedom man," Altagracia replied, cupping my chin in her hand. "I think that makes you a 'don.'"

"Altagracia, how do you say..."

"¿Cómo se dice?" Altagracia interrupted. "You say 'Cómo se dice' when you want to say 'How do you say.' Now, ask me."

"¿Cómo se dice 'name?'"

"¿Cómo se dice 'name' en español?" she repeated. "Se dice 'nombre.'"

"¿Cómo se dice 'friend' en español?"

"Se dice 'amigo.'"

"And 'house?'"

"¿Y 'house?'" she repeated.

"Sí," I answered.

"'House' se dice 'casa.'"

"¿Y 'world?'"

"Mundo."

"¿Y 'flower?'"

"Flor."

"¿Y 'remedy?'"

"Remedio."

"Y, ¿cómo se dice 'to see?'"

"'Mirar.' Another word I have learned in English for 'see' is 'behold.'"

"And poetry?"

"You mean 'pome?'" Altagracia asked.

"No, I mean 'poetry.'"

"Poesía."

I reached into my pocket, felt around in the darkness until I touched the earrings and wrapped my fingers around them. My hand felt hot.

"And 'ear,' Gramita, ¿cómo se dice 'ear?'"

"Oreja."

"¿Y 'queen?'"

"Reina."

I asked Altagracia every word that came to mind on the crest of the hill until the sun moved from 'chicken' all the way to 'God.'

"...And 'earrings,' ¿cómo se dice, Grama?"

"Zarcillos."

"Abuela," I said, "I have something for usted."

I reached into my pocket for the earrings, pulled them out and showed her the zarcillos. They were smaller now. Rolling around in my pocket during the climb, the sharp edges of the salt had smoothed down. Altagracia reached for them slowly. I thought she was going to lift them out of my hand, but instead she cradled my hand in both of hers as though my hand were a priceless chest and the painted salt and flour balls, jewels too precious to be touched.

"¡Oh, mi hijito, qué preciosos!" she exclaimed.

"They are just salt crystals. I made them in class for you, Highgrace."

"Oh, Mío," she said softly, looking deep into my eyes for a few moments, then turning away. "There is not much height left to this old woman, and her grace is almost gone. It will take many, many zarcillos to make me beautiful. Muchos, muchos."

Altagracia looked away from me, and though I couldn't see her face as she spoke, I felt no lack of lonesome.

"Are you alright?" I asked, when she finally turned around to face me.

"Yes, but lonesoming," she answered.

"How come you use that word sometimes, what does it mean?"

"Lonesoming means when your heart turns to sad in Spanish and you don't want it. Soledad we call it, lonesomeness. Like when I think me young in the olden times, in the stories."

"What stories?"

She ignored my question and reached for the zarcillos, but I stopped her.

"No, Gramita, I want to put them on usted. Maybe you could wear them to school when the class does its pomes."

"Oh, they are too precious to wear anywhere else in the world, en todo el mundo, Mío!" Altagracia cried, excitedly. She touched the two crystals as gently as the philosopher mother had brushed her hand past the heads of her two children. Pulling on the strings slowly, she carefully lifted the salt from my hand.

"Let me put them on usted," I repeated.

"Bueno."

Turning her head slightly, Altagracia brushed the tips of her fingers slowly past her cheek, and, like a queen at her crowning, swept away the loose strands of gray that covered her ear.

I looped the string over her ear, and tucked the extra thread out of sight like Mrs. Tandemschnocker had shown us.

"The other oreja, Gramita," I said.

With the same elegance as before, Altagracia turned slowly, ran the back of her hand barely against her cheek and closed her eyes. Without breaking the dream, I gently affixed the last jewel.

I stepped back.

"Behold the rings, su majestad," I said, throwing my arms wide and bowing low.

Altagracia, the Queen, threw her head back and laughed. Her laughter was a bell on the hill.

"¡Gracias, mi señor, my lord, my lord!" she exclaimed, also bowing before me.

"I thought 'señor' meant 'mister.'"

"It does, but it is much, much more than that. It's like 'don.' It means 'sir' or 'lord.'"

"Lord!" I exclaimed. "No one has ever called me 'lord' before!"

"That's because you haven't heard any lord stories."

"Lord stories?"

"Yes. Stories of kings and lords and palaces and Indians that the viejitos used to tell us."

"Viejitos?"

"Old people. And they are at their best in the lord stories. If you ever heard a real storyteller, a cuentacuentos, you would think he was the lord king himself."

"Did you ever see one, a cuentacuentos?"

"Yes, when I was your age. Mame Timia. She was my father's mother, and oh, the stories she told us!"

"Were they actually from the lord times?"

"Yes."

"What were the lord times like? Tell me! Tell me!"

Altagracia's eyes lit up as she reached for her earrings.

God Walked Among Us

"Oh, the lord times. They were a wonderful confusion, they were!" she said, rubbing the salt and closing her eyes to half-smile. "I can see us now, the children. Me. El Belarmín. Zoraida, who we called La Cojita. El Steve..."

"What does La Cojita mean?"

"You'll have to wait for that part," Altagracia said, with a mysterious smile. "That's what Mame Timia would say to us when we got over-anxious ahead of her."

Altagracia returned to the lord times.

"Like I said, it was a wonderful confusion because we traded names, the children of the lord stories and us. There was Belarmín, who was my cousin, but we called him Pedro de Ordimalas, who was from the lord times because he was always playing the rascal among us."

"What do you mean?"

"Well, whatever you told Belarmín to do, he always did the opposite, just like Pedro. They were always playing tricks on everyone they met. El Rey Adobín, King Adobe, was the top king in the lord days. His right-hand man was Juan Maletas, Saddlebag John, and he feared no one. That is until the day he saw himself in an unexpected mirror. Mirrors don't lie, you know, especially when we twist them ourselves."

Altagracia closed her eyes and recalled more people from the times of the adobe king.

"There was El Buen Sarnoso. In English you would call him, Itchy Scab, The Good. None of us wanted to be like him. Then all of us wanted to be like him."

"Why?"

"Well, you see, Itchy Scab, the Good, was friendless."

"With a name like that, who wouldn't be?"

"Exactly. So El Rey Adobín, who, like I said, was the top king because he was so good, took Itchy Scab into his kingdom and had his magicians make a drum for him. And oh, what a drum! With just one beat on it, you could make anything come true."

"Was it made of gold?"

Altagracia laughed.

"No. Flea skin."

"Flea skin!"

"Well, you have to remember this was a flea from the lord times. And there was Rosabra and Sidelia. These were twins born to Juan de los Cíbolos and his wife. They were so poor they could barely afford to feed themselves, let alone two extra mouths."

"So what did they do?"

"They didn't cry."

"What good would that have done?"

"The twins, I mean. They knew right away that if they cried, it would only make things worse for Juan and his poor wife. Her especially. Getting up in the night, feeding, diapers, all that. They wanted to spare their mother all unnecessary work."

Altagracia looked at me and smiled.

"And you know what? For their good intentions, El Rey Adobín gave both of them magical powers when they grew up to be your age."

"Really? What could they do?"

"Oh, all kinds of things. Change river stones into cheese, cheese slices into money. With their magic they provided for Juan and his wife food and wealth far past their living days."

Altagracia adjusted her earrings, then continued.

"There were animals among us then like there are today, and Mame Timia spoke their language. Even now I hear her speaking eagle as she tried to keep Cristal Azul from crossing the arroyo that led to La Suidá de Oro.

"Who was Cristal Azul?"

"He was an over-inquisitive little boy made of blue crystal, and La Suidá de Oro was a city ringing with gold."

"Why wasn't he supposed to cross?"

"Because the owner of that city was an evil man named Tumbatodos, and before anybody entered his city, The Great Toppler gave them a heart of steel. That way, nobody could feel any love for his gold."

"That was smart."

Altagracia looked at me and shook her head.

"No, because once they got the metal heart, they couldn't feel any love, period. And that's why Mame Timia started speaking eagle, to try to keep Cristal Azul from crossing the gully that led to the golden city."

Altagracia looked at me and said, "Pretty smart, don't you think?"

"Yes."

Altagracia reached up, readjusted the salt and continued.

"Indians and their story children also lived among us. Almost always they outwitted their neighbors, los mexicanos. That was us. I remember el Indio Abogado. He was a wise Indian lawyer who won his most important case against a rich man named Don Bernardo who owned a lot of land."

"How."

"With a mere boiled egg."

"For real?"

"Oh, yes. Pulled it right out from under a hen and cooked it."

Altagracia laughed and continued.

"Cajita Astuta was his son. He was our hero."

"What did he do?"

"Cajita Astuta means Little Wise Box, and that's exactly what he was. With a single drop of water, he magnified a speck of sand enough to trap a gold-hungry man named Señor Gachupín Blas."

"How old was he?"

"Oh, your age. There wasn't an Indian in Mame Timia's cuentos that we didn't cheer on. Gets-The-Light was Cajita's brother, I remember. I didn't know it then, but Indian blood is also our blood. Did you know that?"

"No."

"Oh, yes. I realize now that by cheering for Cajita, we were actually cheering for ourselves."

"Am I Indian, Altagracia?"

"Yes. In the blood all of us are, back and forth. And we're Manitos and Manitas, too."

"What are those?"

"'Mano' is short for 'hermano' or brother and 'mana' is short for 'hermana' or sister. Manos and manas are make-believe odd people in the cuentos, but in real life, we also call odd neighbors 'mano' and 'mana.' 'Mana' can be equal to 'doña,' too, however."

"Which is equal to queen, right?" I interrupted.

"Yes."

"So you could be called 'Mana Altagracia?'"

"Yes, if people thought me odd enough. Or queen enough," Altagracia smiled. "Two odd people from the cuentos I remember were

Mano Cacahuate and Mana Cebolla."

"What does that mean?"

"Brother Peanut and Sister Onion. And then came the saints."

"Saints?"

"Yes. San Antonio, San Cristobal, San Isidro. He's the farmer saint. Some saints, like San Tonto, weren't real. Mame Timia made them up. She made things be just by calling out their names, it seems. Like San Tonto. There is no such thing as Saint Idiot, but she could make him be whenever she wanted to use his idiotness to keep us in line. I'm sure he's still a ways from heaven, though."

"What else was there?"

"Well, there was God. Mame Timia made sure He walked among us in her cuentos. But He wasn't a fairy or anything like that who went around giving wishes. He gave advice. Amusing."

Altagracia noticed the confused look on my face.

"Well, not Him. What was amusing is what happened to those who ignored His good advice."

A Balanced Blur

"You see," Altagracia continued, "God is like a board when you step on one end and the other end springs back and hits you. It's just foolishness to go against good advice, because you know before you do it, the other end is just going to come up at you. And death too."

"Death?"

"Yes. Death was powerful like God in the cuentos. Actually, not as powerful, because Mame Timia always put her on level a little lower. God always came out ahead. The name to this day for Death is 'Mi Comadre Sebastiana.'"

"What did she look like?"

"She was black and white, and her fingers were made of river willows. She was always popping in and out. Even in our stories today, she still does. But you want to know something?"

"What."

"She was scary, but she wasn't. Mame Timia knew how to mix her and God just right in her Saddlebag John stories. They balanced out, the two powers, like spices in a cake sitting by the fire in the evening when she told us the stories. We weren't scared. Our dreams were like a blur, balanced."

Altagracia fell silent for a moment, remembering.

"Yes. That's what it was, a balanced blur," she repeated. Again she fell quiet, then, as if addressing herself, she said, "It's hard for me to tell now who was real among us and who wasn't? Was it Pedro de Ordimalas, or el Steve?"

Then, turning to me she said, "Now that I think of it, the blur goes deeper because el Steve was not Steve alone, but Steve, el Ponehuevos."

"Steve, el Ponehuevos?"

"Yes, Steve, the Egglayer. Rather than getting into any fight, even if it was just play fight, he would simply drop to his haunches at the instant of duel and lay there, huddled into himself with his eyes closed."

Altagracia laughed and I joined her.

"The taunting Ponehuevos endured from children even half his age, the chicken. And we never called Zoraida, Zoraida. Remember Zoraida from the beginning, the one you wanted to ask about, La Cojita?"

"Yes."

"Well, here it comes. We always called her La Cojita, because she was born crooked from birth. Poor limpy thing. Everywhere she went, she dragged her left foot. That was good for the rest of us, though. That way, we could track her down for torment. All we had to do was follow her scratches on the rocks along the road."

"That was mean, Altagracia. I can't believe you would..."

"I did do it, and I am sorry now."

"I'm upset with you."

"I am happy you're upset with me. That just shows your heart is gooder than mine when I was your age. Every time I think of it now, I see a board coming up. I wish now I had had a heart like Limpy."

"Why?"

"Because her heart was far from stone. She was always growing things in her hair."

Altagracia noticed the look on my face.

"No, not lice. She was beautiful. In spring she gathered unbloomed willows and made them flower in her hair. All summer long, there were more daisies on her head than in the meadow. Even in autumn when everything starts to fade, she kept her color."

"What do you mean?"

"Oh, it was wonderful. One day she came in wearing an apple rind."

Altagracia stretched out her arms.

"It was this long. She salvaged it from the pile where her mother was making winter jelly. That rind kept her going all through fall when Dead Man Winter, El Zozobra showed up. And even he couldn't keep her from flowering, though he used all his powers to depress like dangling ice from every window."

"But how? There aren't any flowers in winter."

"For Limpy there were. She would sit down with a shopping catalog and scour the color pages for muñequitas."

"What's ..."

"I'm getting there. Muñequitas is paper dollies. She cut them into strips. Then, taking her scissors, one blade of them, she rasped each shred of doll until it was curled kinky. Then she pinched all the colors together and made little flowers. She put these in her hair and fed the hunger in her head until spring came up again."

Altagracia smiled, remembering, then continued.

"El Steve, The Egglayer. Pedro de Ordimalas. Talking Eagles. Indians."

She sighed.

"Me."

She looked out over Verdistancia in the haze.

"We all lived in a city of gold," she continued, "mixed together in the divine, playing to the beat of a flea-skinned drum. What was real? What was imagined?"

Altagracia reached for the earrings and rubbed them slowly. Then, as if she were alone on the mountain and addressing the air over Verdistancia, she continued. "No one questioned what was real, and what wasn't..." Her voice trailed off.

"Verdistancia," she whispered.

Then, after a long moment of silence, she returned to pick up her voice, "...like now, sitting in the divine mixture wondering what is true and what is not."

"What does Verdistancia mean?

"Well, like I said.."

"Green distance," I interrupted. "What else does it mean?"

"To see distance," she said.

Falling silent, she looked out into the green-tinged distance in the haze blow us.

"Volviendo a Verdistancia," she said to herself, "returning to Verdistancia." Then, after a long moment and as if becoming aware of me, she said, "For a moment I saw myself returning to Verdistancia. If you want, someday I can tell you all about Mana Onofre and Mana Lines and all the other viejitos from when I was a girl. How would you like that?"

"I would like it. Who were Mana Onofre and Mana Lines?"

"Mame Timia's sisters. They were curanderas, healers," she said, gazing back into the village in the haze.

The Indian's Pebbles

"Altagracia," I said, almost afraid to enter into her world and break her away from the viejitos in her mind, "If I am Indian in the blood a little, you could tell me an Indian story now."

Altagracia looked at me and smiled as she had during Limpy's heart.

"Do you really want me to?" she asked.

"Yes."

"How about Las Piedritas del Indio?"

"What does it mean?"

"It means The Indian's Pebbles. It's about Cajita's father who later went on to be the wise lawyer, remember?"

"Yes. Did he have a feather crown?"

"You mean a bonnet? Yes. He was a big chief."

"Like the one on my tablet?"

"Yes."

"Were the chiefs like kings with their jewelly crowns, only feathery?"

"What do you mean?"

"The big chiefs, I mean. The more feathers they had, the more importanter they were. Isn't that how it was?"

"That's how it was."

"Tell me about the big chief."

"Fine, but I am going to make it very short because we need to be getting off this mountain. Someday you can make the story longer if you want. You can move the embers around it. That's what Mame Timia used to tell us."

"Go!"

"Alright," Altagracia said, rubbing the salt as if consulting the earrings. "Way back in the lord times and eagles and us, there was an Indian who lived by a rich, but very stingy neighbor. A vecino cusco, we would say. And he was hungry. One day he went to visit him and found him having supper because it was late. When the indio knocked at the door, his vecino cusco told him to come in and sit down, but that he had to sit away from the table. Well, as the vecino cusco ate without inviting him, the Indian decided he would teach his stingy neighbor a lesson. "Vecino, he said, how much do you think a bolita de oro as big as a cherry would be worth?" The vecino cusco, without looking up from his plate answered. "Oh, a little ball of gold the size of a cherry would be worth a little something, I suppose. It's only a pebble." Then the indio responded, "And what would a bolita the size of a cirgüela be worth?" "A bolita the size of a plum?" asked the vecino cusco, looking up with interest from his plate, soup still dripping from his moustache. "Well, that would be worth some pretty good pesitos."

Altagracia interrupted her story and explained. "'Pesitos' means pretty dollars."

She reached up to the earrings, and continued.

"Then the Indian put his two fists together into the size of the man's heart and said, "And a bolita this size?" At that moment the vecino cusco pushed his chair back and said, "Look, friend, why don't you pull up your chair and let's talk about it over dinner." The indio pulled his chair to the table and the vecino cusco served him. Then, he served himself and the two ate. Twice, when the Indian had eaten everything on his plate, the vecino cusco pushed more meat and fruit in his direction. When the vecino cusco saw that the indio had eaten his full and had pushed his plate back, he said, "Now, brother, where did you say you had gold as big as your fist?" "I didn't," replied the indio. "I was only asking in case someday I should stumble across some." And that is how Cajita's father educated his stingy neighbor."

"I am glad the hungry Indian won," I said.

"Yes," Altagracia said, "but think again. Who was the hungry man, the Indian or the vecino cusco? Run the story through your mind again."

Altagracia waited, rubbing the salt slowly as I ran my mind through the story.

Viejitos Revisited, Possibilities

"The man who had everything was hungrier."

"Why?"

"Because..," I said enthusiastically.

"Never mind," Altagracia interrupted, "I know that you know. I see it in your eyes."

"What do you see?"

"That you have an Indian heart."

I smiled.

"Do you think I could tell that Indian story in Mrs. Tandemschnocker's class when the class does its pomes?"

"Oh, absolutely!" Altagracia said, picking up a stick and clearing a patch of dirt over a scattering of leaves beside her. "And after you tell it you can even write it if you want. And when you write it, put your name to it like this."

She scratched the clearing with the stick, eyed the scratches for a moment, then re-raked the ground and said, "And after you write it, make sure you put in some important wigglies under your name, like that. Writers always do."

"But I can't read it," I said, tossing a handful of dry leaves over her pretend signature.

"That's fine," she said laughing, "because I can't write it either."

"And what if they don't like it? I mean, if I write a book?"

"They? Don't matter. We will mint our own medals, and calligraphy our own awards. Autores del futuro. Here, you try it."

"What's...?"

"Here, you try it," she said, interrupting me and handing me the stick.

I traced the twig along the tiny furrows she had made and handed it back to her.

"No. You need to put in your own wiggles."

Carefully, I squeezed the stick along the edge of the clearing and the border of leaves without disturbing them and rubbed it back and forth.

"Feels kind of important signing your name all mysterious-like, don't it?"

"Yes," I answered, wondering what she would say if I told her of the many times I had already done it in Mrs. Tandemschnocker's class without trying, and how she had told me to write my name so she could read it.

"The Indian story was only one of the stories Mame Timia told me when I was your age. She also knew a sumillion adivinanzas."

"What are avinanzas?"

"Adivinanzas are riddles, entire pictures in a single drop. Mame Timia used to tell me pounds and pounds of them. Some day I'll tell you them. I won't tell you any now, because those take a lot of time and we need to be getting off this mountain. For adivinanzas, you have to think a lot before you figger them out. Actually, I think riddles are poesía of the mind."

"Tell me one, just a little drop one to see if I can figger it out."

"Fine, just one, because we need to be getting home."

Altagracia thought for a moment, then she said, "I'll tell you my favorite. I think it's the most beautiful adivinanza in Spanish. It's about a doncella, a beautiful young girl dressed in nothing but blue and white. She is walking around on the balcony of heaven looking down and shining like a star. Of course when you hear it you have to guess it's the moon."

La Bella Doncella

A smile came across Altagracia's face as she opened the riddle bottle and rhymed.

"Por las barandas del cielo se pasea una doncella, vestida de azul y blanco, reluciendo como estrella."

"That sounded almost like music."

"Many adivinanzas are music. I used to tell that adivinanza to Risa all the time when she was your age and well, well past. She liked to hear it over and over, the sound of it, the rhyming, even though she knew the answer. That and the Indian story."

"Por las brasas..." I said, trying to repeat the riddle, but Altagracia's laughter interrupted me.

"You haven't said the adivinanza," she said, laughing. "You've just said, 'Through the ashes...'"

"Don't laugh, Altagracia, I'm just trying to make the picture in my mind."

"Well, you're going to have to practice for a good while because to bring an adivinanza alive takes quite some time."

"I mean the picture of my mother."

Instantly, as if having stepped on the end of a board, Altagracia flashed pale, and fell silent.

"Mío," Altagracia said, softly, "Risa."

She reached for me.

"Risa..." I said, throwing my arms around my Gramita's waist, my mother, searching for her face in what seemed a hundred going on ten thousand. Burying my face deep into her apron, I whispered the music words over and over among the faded roses....

"Mío..."

I heard Altagracia's voice calling me from above.

"What?" I asked, looking up and seeing her in the blue crowned with clouds.

"I'll give you the adivinanzas so you can make all the pictures you want when we get home," she said, as I faced back into the apron. "All of them."

"All of them?" I asked, from the faded flowers where I was, still trying to put my mother together in my mind with riddle pictures.

"All that I know. All that Mame Timia told me that the Rey Adobín told her," Altagracia said from the vapor. "The bottle is full of them. They are all very old. Viejitas. You can write them in a book if you want to. They are poetry under the ashes still burning. Viejitos revisited offer many possibilities."

I accepted Altagracia's offer of my mother's pictures in the blur of her apron. I rested in the flowers, buried, thinking up my mother while Altagracia waited for me.

Finally, with all the imagined photographs of my mother in place, I looked up at Altagracia and said, "I liked the avinanza as much as my mother, Altagracia."

"Good."

"I liked everything. Everything that the Rey Adobín talked into the bottle and how he told it to Mame Timia, and she told it to you and you, my mother."

Altagracia pressed me against her.

"But you still have the secret thoughts you haven't told me, and your high poetry, remember? And you can't break a promise."

I didn't wait for her to answer. Hugging her, I buried my face back into her apron and waited.

I Can Hear God Laughing

"High poetry?" she asked.

With my face still deep in the faded roses, I could hear Altagracia's voice falling on me like a curtain from beyond the clouds.

"Sí, you know, the secret thought which God answers without you having to ask Him."

Altagracia remained quiet for a few moments. She is not going to tell me, I thought.

"Remember, Abuela, you're not supposed to break a promise," I muffled into the old apron.

I breathed in. Altagracia's apron smelled of familiar bread.

"I won't," I heard her say. "I think high poetry is happening ahora mismo, Mío, right now. At this moment, Dios is answering my secret thought. If I tell you my two thoughts, will you promise not to tell anyone?"

"Swear to die."

Again, Altagracia was quiet. It seemed as though she were afraid to tell me. I pulled my face out of her apron, and looked directly up at her.

"Grama!" I half-threatened, "I'm telling you swear to die I'll never tell anybody! Now, tell me!"

"Bueno, I will tell you."

I closed my eyes and went back to the roses.

"Mío," she began slowly, placing a hand under my chin and saying each word carefully, "remember when I told you how beautiful it was back in the olden times when the cherry shined?"

I nodded.

"My two secret thoughts start way back when I was young, almost in the yester. Remember I told you how everybody worked hard and that even for children, work was their school?"

"Sí."

"Well, that's all the school I ever had, hard work. I have wished for a long time I could have gone to school, Mío. There were no books then, only work. Mio, I never learned to read or write."

Altagracia's words fell on me like a cloud of lead.

"What! Granma, I didn't know you didn't know!"

"And now, how I wish I could! I see so many things around me."

"Poesia?"

"Sí, to write poesía."

"How come you are so smart then, if you don't know how to read or write? Where did you get all your poesía?"

"You don't have to know how to read or write to know poesía. Dios sends it when you ask. Sometimes in the rainbow, sometimes in the weeping willow, remember? That's the only way to poesía. Some pomers who are wiser than me will probably disagree because they have been trained to pome, but I don't know."

"And what is your other thought?"

"That one is much more hidden. It's between Dios and me, but not even He knows it."

"What is it, Altagracia?"

She hesitated even more than before.

"Grama! I sweared, remember? Don't be afraid to tell me. I double promise and eat a worm I won't tell!"

I felt Altagracia hold me tighter.

"Mío," she said slowly, "I fight with Dios a lot."

"What? Dios? I thought you loved Dios."

"Sí, amo a Dios. I do love God, Mío, mucho, mucho, but who walk with God, walk alone."

"What do you mean?"

"Well, remember way back before we began climbing the loma, just before I saw you sitting on the food bench under the tree? I couldn't tell anyone about it nor hold it back any more. I think maybe I made Him a little mad. No sé, I'm not sure. I just blurted it out."

"What do you mean? Blurted what out?"

"I kept thinking the same thing over and over all morning. 'Spring,' I thought, 'beautiful spring, la primavera, linda, linda. Here it is again! And here I am también, not being able to write any of it.'"

"I still don't understand."

"Mío, I just kept thinking it, until point blank I thought it out in anger with my mouth."

"Thought what out?"

"I shouted at Dios, Mío! In my anger, in the middle of such a beautiful spring I yelled out, '¡De qué me sirve tanta poesía, Oh Señor mi Dios, si todo lo que me dejas trabajar es este cavador! No puedo escribir nada.'"

"Altagracia, I didn't understand anything you said, except Dios y poesía. Tell me in English."

Altagracia hesitated again.

I said, "What good is all this poetry, Oh, Lord, my God, if all You're going to let me handle is this hoe! I can't write any of it!"

There were tears in Altagracia's eyes. The feeling of the black girl by the sea covered me all over, immensely. I heard the crack of stones in my pocket. The veined one she had given me while climbing the hill moved. The sadness in Altagracia's eyes pushed me deep under. The ocean was bearing all its weight down on the tiny breast of my conch. I couldn't breathe.

"Oh, Mío, por muchos años, for many years I have rolled that thought around and around in my heart, but today I thought it out in anger. By this afternoon I found myself hitting the earth so hard and opening it up so much that many of the seeds landed too deep. I am sure a lot of the tiny ones, los rábanos y mis pobres zanahorias— yes, especially the radishes and my poor carrots—they are not going to come up. I even found myself chopping away at the same weed even after I had hoed it down. My lips were salt after that. I actually talked to God in anger. I didn't just think it."

Altagracia was quiet for a moment, then she began to cry.

"Sal," she said. "Salt. I used salt with God."

"I don't think you made Him mad," I said, hugging her.

She looked at me. Behind the water, I could see great hope in her eyes.

"Are you sure?" she asked, almost as if I were both, teacher and answer.

"I am sure, Gramita. And I am also sure the senioras and the roobanoes will find their way up."

Altagracia chuckled at my Spanish.

"Mío," Altagracia began, slowly, "you know what?"

"What?"

"I am beginning to think you're right."

"What do you mean?"

"I can hear God laughing in my ear, ahora mismo. Right now He is answering me without me even asking."

"I don't understand."

"Earlier this afternoon on the food bench. Remember how we were both low before we started climbing the loma? Now look at us.

Here we are. On top of the hill! I hear God laughing! I can write, Mío, I can write!"

"What do you mean?"

I felt my Gramita reach down and put both hands firmly on my head.

"Mío!" she exclaimed as she pressed me together, "¡Dios me ha dado una pluma!"

She squeezed my head closer, as if putting me in her pocket and repeated, "God has given me a pen!"

The Water Has To Mold the Glass

"We've talked above the clouds for what seems years," Altagracia said, pointing to where the sun was setting. "If we don't start for home soon, we'll have to feel our way down."

"Just follow the road."

"Or, I'll sing you up the moon and cut across," she said, laughing. "Grampo should be home by now. I hope he was able to get Tumbaga penned. He's the only one who can handle that ram."

"I know. He doesn't like anybody near his sheep."

"He would have already sold that horned brute except for his pelt. That ram coats out more wool than any two put together."

Altagracia glanced in the direction of Grampo's quarry. "Yes, I'm sure he's home by now. Even though the days are getting longer, the quarry is too dark to be working now. But who knows? As good as he and Cesario are at digging rock and setting it, what's the dark of night to them?"

"I know. Who's older, Grampo or Cesario."

"Grampo is. Cesario is the youngest of the five brothers."

"Why do they call him Cesario Penitente?"

"Penitente means someone who works hard at a loss for God. Someday, I'll tell you about the Penitentes."

"Is that why he moves rocks?"

"Could be. Only the three of them know. God, him, and the stones. I just know that Grampo taught him all he knows about stone."

I thought of Grampo and his brother as I walked beside Altagracia. The two were always working, always wrestling rocks, it seemed. I had gone several times to the quarry where they pried the flat stones loose, piedra laja, Grampo called them, but the only thing I liked about it was riding the horses up and the loaded wagons down.

"You haven't said anything for a while," Altagracia asked, from the now dark road. "¿Estás cansado?"

"What?"

"Are you tired?

"No, I was just thinking."

"Most of the time that's good," she replied with a chuckle.

"What I'm trying to figger out is, when I write poesía for Mrs. Tandemschnocker, how am I going to do it?"

"I don't understand what you mean."

"Well, what if I see poetry in Spanish, and I want to write it for Mrs. Tandemschnocker? How do I do that without turning it into English?"

Altagracia didn't answer, but even in the darkness, I knew she was already figuring it out.

"I see what you mean," she finally replied.

Surrounded by twinkles of light, we continued in silence. Every now and then, a near-by owl hooted, sounding far away but actually very near, maytricking us with every call. On either side of us, I could hear the noises of the night world scamper aside to let us pass.

We walked through several stars. Finally, from somewhere near the moon, Altagracia broke the silence. Reaching out, she placed her hand on my arm and brought me to a stop.

"Let me ask you something."

"What is it?"

"Remember when I told you you can't take poetry and pen it up in a pome?"

"Sí."

"Why do you think that is?"

"I don't know."

"Because poesía is water, that's why. And like agua, God meant it free."

"What do you mean?"

"Water has no shape. Have you ever thought of that? Something you can see and touch and yet can't hold because it has no shape?"

I didn't answer.

"But you can bend it. Water takes the shape of whatever you put it in, a goblet or a jug."

"What's a goblet?"

"A goblet is a rich man's liquor jug. Now, let me ask you. If you take water that's draping a clear skirt over the lip of a round fountain, and put it in a fat glass, what do you get?"

"Grama! I asked you a serious question!" I replied sharply, looking at her, but seeing only silhouette where she blotted out the stars. "You would get a glass of water, of course!"

109

"No. You would get a glass of fat water. Why? Because the container molds the water. You would get fat water, not true water."

"So?"

"So, that is how I would answer your Tandemschnocker question. If you see poesía en español, you must keep it that— poesía en español, true. You must not change it to fit the pome. If you do, you'll get a fat pome."

"You mean talk Spanish in English?"

"Sí, or the other way around, if that's what you see."

"Are you sure?"

"Sí. The water, el agua, has to mold the glass."

"What do you mean?"

"Mío, you now have two tongues, dos lenguas. From now on, you will see the world through two different windows. Dos mundos. Many times the words of one do not fit through the opening of the other, and so the frame has to mold itself to the view. It can't be the other way around."

"What is 'dos mundos?'"

"'Dos mundos' is two worlds. And people who live in two worlds do not live in either, but in the middle."

"Dos mundos? Two worlds?" I asked.

"Yes. And you are the balance. One mundo in one hand and another mundo in the other."

"A balance? Is that like weight?"

"Yes. Living on the needle. Balancing the furies."

Altagracia placed her hand on my shoulder and said, "Mío, you are one of us now."

Altagracia in the Window

Several weeks later, the class read its pomes. People were sitting wherever they could, on the floor, on the bookshelves. Mrs. Tandemschnocker had cleared her desk and seven people had crowded themselves onto it. She had removed her world from the corner of her desk and had wedged it into the broom closet where she kept all her old tests. Two men sat on the sacred corner.

Mrs. Tandemschnocker called on everyone to introduce themselves before they read.

She called my name.

I stood up, walked to the front of the room, and faced the crowd. Sitting on the floor close to my feet and looking up at me was the mother with the skinned knees. She had a philosopher on either leg, each content with his half lap.

I could see Altagracia sitting on a window ledge at the very back of the room. Unnoticed and almost shyly she had entered and seated herself right next to the door. She appeared ready to leave at any moment. Sunlight filled her window and surrounded her. Light coming through the open door fell on her earrings and constantly changed the colors on the crystals. Every ray that fell on them gave her many, many earrings, a different pair every time she moved her head.

I reached into my pocket and pulled out water, poesía.

I looked again in the direction of Altagracia.

I was standing, she was sitting. I looked at her through the sun. There was silence. She could not talk to me because she was far, far away. Sitting lightly on the edge and holding the window sill with both hands, she reminded me of migrants in the angelus of the evening. She was among the tired ones on the work trough who held the water's edge for one last moment right before going home.

She nodded and smiled at me to introduce myself.

"Soy Mío, y soy mío.
Cuando soy mío y sé mi nombre,
soy la flor del mundo.
I am Mío, and I am my own.
When I am mine and know my name,
I am the flower of the world."

I glanced in the direction of Highgrace through the mist of rays.
She smiled again and nodded for me to continue. As she rested in sanctuary, a glimpse of sunlight glinted off the salt I had given her. The sun moved, the glint became a shower of rays, and Altagracia vanished into the sun.
I bowed my head and read.

Treehouses

Everyone needs a treehouse
because there is always
no lack of lonesome,
mi Gramita says.
We built a treehouse
beside the stream
with wood still good
from the Old Place,
mi Gramita y yo.
We made the steps short because
little old abuelitas have to climb, too.
There, water unspools itself forever
falling over the tumble of rocks
under the twisting oak going up.
Remedies grow wild there
because the water is good,
Indian remedios.
Agua es water.
On two flat flagstones,
piedra laja, and foursquare strong,
Altagracia called them,
we planted two long kiva poles
we took from the Old Place.
Like two wooden arms,
they hold the slats between them,

each board a weathered horizon leading upward.
It's always dark underneath,
because
the light is on top.
Indians always go up when they go down
into the dark hole to pray.
Where the tree ends and the sky begins,
there the sheep poles rest,
two canes hooked on the forearm
of the ancient giant whose
bark spirals higher and higher.
I reach out both arms
and place them
on the poles of heaven's ladder.
Holding the two rails firmly and
looking up, my arms grow
until they converge immensely
high on my Gramita's doorway
where the doormat is free of dust.
There it is, my Gramita's casa,
pieces of sky and goat boards
laced together with light.
Air holds everything together.
Tangled in the green and veiled in hope,
my best amigo, Blue Boy,
flies from limb to limb...
Birds build treehouses like poesía
with only pajama strings and old grass.
Casas,
we build them new,
houses, like rows and rows of pomes.
We plant and plant shrubs around them,
even set out goblets of water
hoping to coax poesía
like we would a bird,
but poesía will not come to live with us.
It will not live hedged in.
And so,
trained to pome and
maytricked,
we live alone.

In our beautiful yards,
our trees go from green to ground
and there is no gold.
We walk on our food.
Like wardrobes on a clothesline we hang.
Our vanes turn like angry angels.
There are holes in our sleep, now...

Stirring Altagracia's Embers

...now, swimming in the reflections of Mary Constable's window, I still hear the applause breaking out in Mrs. Tandemschnocker's room long before I finished. The loudest came from the two philosophers at my feet who were clapping on each other's hands.

"Is there more?" Mrs. Tandemschnocker asked, from where she sat across the room. She was shouting through the applause.

"I still have the Indian story, Big Chief!" I shouted, trying to make myself heard.

Mrs. Tandemschnocker shook her head.

"Big Chief!" I called out, louder. "I still have Big Chief and other stories from the earrings!"

Mrs. Tandemschnocker cupped her hand around her ear and waved her finger back and forth. She motioned for someone else to stand up because she could not hear me through the trembling air...

...the trembling air and the distorted light coming through the sun-bleached window of the thrift shop become one and I hear Mrs. Tandemschnocker calling from the direction of the canning jars. A reflection now, she makes her way toward me through the webbed light.

Without a word and still the teacher, she sits beside me. She looks over my shoulder, but, before she can invite herself to my paper, I place the tablet in her hand.

For a moment she and Big Chief stare at each other.

She flips the tablet over and opens it to the last page where she always went first.

"Don't forget your name," she says, flipping it back to the front cover.

She studies Big Chief's eyes for a moment, then carefully folds the red and black feathers of his bonnet backward to the first written page and begins to read.

Big Chief

"This happens in the times of lord," Mrs. Tandemschnocker began to read out loud, as she always did.

Then she dropped to a whisper, "Acy was a beautiful man, and Taracahi knew it. Taracahi was hungry, and Acy knew it."

Mrs. Tandemschnocker looked up from the tablet, glanced at me briefly, then continued to read silently.

Though Taracahi had invested the greater part of the morning following the quail tracks, always a hill ahead of him, the leather-lean Yaqui would not despair. Taracahi had known from the time his father, Cajita, had taken him out on his first hunt that the desert yielded up food only in proportion to the energy invested. Sometimes less.

"Point your energy," the big chief had said. "Tracking is more a matter of waiting than walking."

The quail tracks dropped into the arroyo, and Taracahi followed. He walked cautiously along the almost invisible sand prints of the bird. He stopped and fell to his knees for a closer look. The quail, sensing danger though still far behind, left the soft sand for the larger pebbles along the bank. The debris overwhelmed the tiny marks to the point of fading from Taracahi's acute eyes, but the sapient youth knew that his survival rested on two things.

"Your mental poise behind the tracks," Cajita had told him, "and maintaining control over the torque of hunger in your stomach will determine if you eat, and when."

The astute youth lowered his head to the eye level of the bird. Hoping to catch a glimpse of the tiny dangling crown of red fluff, he eyed the underbrush. Judging from the trajectory of the track's direction, his prey was moving toward the purple-gray of a distant mesa. The young Yaqui knew the bird would allay its hunger on the juice of lemitilla berries ripening on the butte's side. Knowing the grove was still a hot hour away, the sagacious Yaqui decided to allow the fowl time to reach and feast the thicket. Time and patience were his allies. If he waited long enough, the acidic juice would work its wine and he would save an arrow.

Silence and Water

Prudence told the sapient youth now that he would do well to conserve his strength. He should return to the hollow under the arroyo embankment. There, by the outcropping of water, he should await the mid-day simmering to subside.

Hunger twisted in his stomach, but Taracahi obeyed.

He would eat water until evening, and then the quail.

Backtracking quietly, his head shielded under the tatters of his shirt to conserve liquid and prevent further sapping of strength, he finally reached the desert rivulet where he had drunk last. The tiny trickle, a residue from a flash of torrents past, licked out barely from beneath a sandstone ledge. Flowing a few inches before consuming downward in the arroyo sand, the meager flow nourished a few scant shrubs and some dwarf willows.

Deer, quietly, came to drink at the small water. Coyotes, too, cunning, gathered here with their young. After drinking their fill, they sniffed long where the deer had stood and hooked their musk. Embedding the scent firmly in their common conscious, the wily animals danced before the hunt. Flashing each other with smiles and carvings beautiful with teeth, they tailed and necked into each other gathering passion for the kill. Interwoven they swirled locked, snarling their love. Their cunning shared and of one brain, they pulled apart momentarily, then, like saliva thirsty for itself and barkless, they came together again. One, the leader, sniffed the underbrush, found the deer print, and nosed into it. The pack followed, a magnet inseparable from the steel.

Prey and predator gone and the silent water safe, lizard, who had watched from beneath the ledge, exited to drink. Peering cautiously at first, the tiny sauria slipped out blade-thin from between shadow and stone. It paused at the water trickle. With its threadlet tongue barely exiting its mouth and both eyes upward for desert hawks, in an instant, it lapped up several flashes. Then, its body still pointing streamward, its feet millipede fast, it traced its steps backwards, and as quickly as it appeared, disappeared.

Silence and water.

The cycle of the desert that powers the species.

Some living.

Some dying.

Some watching water turn to meat, meat to milk...and finally, in time, milk back to water again when, unable to keep attachment to the deer tracks, they return their juices to the sand.

Tituli Yaqui

When Taracahi arrived at the trickle, lizard was asleep between the layers of stone. From the water's edge near his bed, a desert willow draped a leaf-strung limb over the rivulet. From the opposite shore, another necklace arched out gracefully from beneath the cool and matched it. In the intense heat, the tiny flow emerged, traveled a few inches, swirled a small profusion of sand in a tiny pool, exited, and disappeared. Beyond the pebble line dividing wet and dry, the desert burned.

Taracahi leaned one hand on the ledge. Lowering himself prone above the water as lizard had, he drew his face to the surface.

Above him, the sun seared.

Before his tongue touched the cool, he was tasting it in his mouth and beyond.

In his stomach tight with hunger.

On his burning back.

In his brain.

Lip close to the vein of water he saw the sky, molten blue riding the tiny ripple of his drink, reflected on the water. He watched as the sun rays stirred the sands in the crucible of stone. Though the bottom was a scant inch from the surface, the concavity cradling the swirls appeared deep, an infinity of blue away.

The sky will feed my hunger, he said to himself, prudence.

Taracahi reached his tongue to the drop of water flowing by. As it touched the liquid point, the sun, halting its arc across the sky, stirred the waters with a ray. A sudden glint in the interswirling caught Taracahi's eye.

The blues converged.

Water and sky spoke.

Taracahi was their word.

Instantly, the sun pulled up and the water flowed.

Taracahi's eyes were opening.

On the mesa, the quail reached the lemitilla grove as the berries peaked in power.

It began to feed.

Pushing himself up arm-straight, the vigilant Yaqui stared at the water, into it, and beyond.

The glint was gone, lost in the gyrations of the grains.

Taracahi cocked his head and the glint appeared, still anchored in the swirling grit.

On the mesa, the quail pecked at several grains of sand, chose the brilliant one, and added the sparkle to his gizzard stones.

Taracahi cocked his head again, and the glint melted into a liquid grinding of particles and water.

Taracahi lowered himself image-close above the flow as the quail returned to feast the berried ground.

The point of light was still there, burning under water, diminished now in the angle of the flow, now greatly magnified by the sun raying in the water. He withdrew slightly back and forth over the silver-blue and the golden speck disappeared and reappeared. In the ripples, the grain turned pliant and stretched, liquefaction in the flow. It was only sunlight swirling yellow around common sand.

Reaching out a hand, Taracahi dammed the trickle. The water stopped an inch downstream, and immediately, the burning desert closed in. Upstream, the rivulet swelled into a clear lens. The quiet of the shallow, magnified the speck into a nugget.

Taracahi removed his hand, the golden grain turned to water, but hunger kept his eye on the point. No sand could swirl enough to move it from the ray providence had sprouted for him at the bottom of the pool.

Hunger torqued in his stomach again, but, recalling Cajita, Taracahi overrode it. The sun above and the sun in the water are one, he thought, they have spoken. I must find their word.

Prone, face to the surface, Taracahi studied the grain, recalling Cajita's lessons. Cajita was a man of gold, he thought, wise and true. His words were gold, and they could make this gold real if he tracked it long enough.

Taracahi continued tracking the sun rays through the water. Face to the mirror he traveled, discerning between clouds reflected on the water and flash of flow below. Suddenly, as if seeing Cajita among the reflections, he stopped.

His eyes were opened.

Taracahi smiled.

This gold was food.

Balancing on one hand, Taracahi reached slowly through the waters and the stirring sands, as if toward a sleeping quail. His eyes and fingers were one. Silently they glided, coyotes on the track, stealing upon the water spirit that slept gleaming on its bed. Though the water rippled away the nugget, Taracahi kept his gaze on the point where the water had vaporized the glint. Unblinking through the grinding sands he waited for the water to ripple in his favor. The instant providence sluiced in his direction and the nugget reappeared, his fingers and his eyes fused anew, and, coyote cunning, started through the clear flux. Cajita's lessons, unblinking in stealth, were steering him well through the confusing sands. That and hunger.

Taracahi's finger pounced upon the sacred grain he knew would turn his quail golden.

"Yaqui!" he cried jubilant.

"Yaqui!" echoed the stillness round and round, away, away rejoicing.

Taracahi kept his finger pressed against the grain, a coyote, his weight upon the struggling deer, waiting for his mate. Carefully Taracahi crept his thumb through the flow in the direction of the floundering gold. He waited for the precise ripple,. Then suddenly, the mate lunged at the deer's throat. Taracahi closed his thumb against his finger and surrounded the golden germ.

"Tituli!" he cried.

"Tituli!" rang the silence.

With the sperm of life clasped tightly, Taracahi backtracked carefully through the water. Then, in a splashing up of water, he burst his hand out from the pool in the profuse spurting that turns spirit into newborn flesh.

"Tituli Yaqui! Tituli Yaqui!" he cried.

"Beautiful Yaqui! Beautiful Yaqui!" the silence sang.

The lizard, awakened by Taracahi's jubilance and sandwiched still between shadow and stone, peeked its point face through.

Taracahi looked at his fist glistening silver-tense under the sun.

Would his sun be there?

He opened his hand. Cradled in his palm was the flash of gold, weightless, an infant barely fleshed and wrapped in gauze, asleep.

But it would grow.

Taracahi knew it.

His eyes, always on Cajita, were open now, and Cajita was a man of gold. Already he was nourishing his hunger.

On the far mesa a drop of blood dangling as crown and fed to fatness on the yellow berries, the quail closed his eyes, and, as if drunk on gold, fell asleep.

The Trail Again

Sitting by the silent water under the meager bower of the willow his hand an open plate before him, Taracahi smiled at his weightless food. He pushed the grain gently with his finger, coaxing it to smile up at him as he had smiled up at Cajita from the blanket when, still fresh in the blood, the Yaqui chief had pulled him forth.

The lizard, as if to get a closer look at Taracahi's child, slipped the shadow and edged himself down the ledge. Mottled from shades not fully shrugged, it edged along the stream, half in half out. Shedding black for blue but blackly-veined still, it stole its way beside Taracahi, and climbed the willow's arch. From its slender perch behind Taracahi, it watched, shifting colors in the sway. Blue to clouded white and shadow, to speckled shade, then to clear black.

With his free hand, Taracahi reached into the running trickle, dipped a finger in the flow, and retrieved a drop. As if molten glass, he carefully balanced the liquid on his nail and suspended it above the grain.

Taracahi smiled as he watched the sun trembling in the sphere.

He lowered the burning water gently, and as it touched the particle, the sun-filled drop magnified it into gold.

Hunger twisted in his stomach

Taracahi raised the drop above the speck and lowered it again. The gold loomed enormous, a loaf of bread a hundredfold.

His eyes had been opened.

Closing his hand on the speck, he rose from the ledge with quail in hand, and set off in the direction of La Zarza.

Lizard, abandoned in the sky, swayed alone. Then, hugging its way backward down the willow, it made its way through the silent oasis to the ledge's foot. There, spread-legging himself against the wall, he twisted himself upward clawing the stone face as he rose. He reached his bed of shade. The sun, higher by many levels now, arced one degree, shifted the shadow of the ledge, and shrouded him in black.

The Ivy

It was early evening when Taracahi scaled the sides of the arroyo and approached La Zarza, the hacienda where Cajita had spent seasons picking Don Amado's fruit.

Hunger twisted in his stomach as Taracahi walked through the orchard, but he made no effort for an apple, though they brushed him in the face.

Acy, Don Amado's heir, saw him coming. Resting under the ivy of the patio blooming red, he made little effort at movement in his lounge.

Taracahi raised a palm in Acy's direction greeting him as he approached, but Acy kept his quiet.

Without breaking stride, Taracahi raised it a second time.

Again Acy went unmoved.

Taracahi advanced and raised it third time, wishing to believe Acy had not seen his previous two greetings.

Acy did not return the greeting.

By now, Taracahi was a few feet from the patio where Acy rested on the ivy draped bench.

He raised his hand a fourth time and Acy returned the greeting.

Cajita was right, thought Taracahi, as he stood now by the patio's edge and looked upon the stranger. Acy is a beautiful man.

Taracahi looked into Acy's eyes. Inherited from his mother, they were blue-green quiet and flecked with amber. His skin, cream-brown tinged slightly by the sun, was as Cajita had described Don Amado. Taracahi looked at Acy's wrists. They were sculptured delicate and white where his gloves shielded them.

"Señor," Taracahi said, unsure of the strange language and the foreign landscape before him.

"Sí, what is it," Acy replied, without stirring in his nest. Then, thinking himself master, he continued. "No, there's no work. All the fruit has been picked."

"Señor," Taracahi said, offering a closed fist in Acy's direction.

"I know you're strong, but I'm telling you, there's no work."

"Señor," Taracahi persisted, adding weight to his fist.

Acy, on the point of flight, hesitated momentarily, then answered. "What is it?

Acy shifted slightly in the nest.

Taracahi noticed a nibble of interest in his voice, and nodded.

"What do you have?" Acy asked, rising to one elbow on the ivy bed.

Taracahi added more weight to his hand and Acy felt it.

He rose from the nest.

He took a step toward Taracahi and said, "You have something for me?" Then, feigning disinterest, he turned around and walked toward the door behind him.

"You can come back tomorrow. I don't have time right now. Dinner is waiting and cold beans don't belong in a man's body."

"Señor!" Taracahi called after him.

Acy stopped.

Taracahi sensed a wavering in Acy as he stood half-way through the door.

Acy was a bird struggling, caught between escape and further feeding.

"Señor," Taracahi repeated.

Acy turned, stepped off the doorway in Taracahi's direction.

Taracahi smiled. He would not have to use an arrow.

"Señor," Taracahi said, motioning with baited fist for Acy to accompany him to a bird bath on the patio's edge.

Acy obeyed.

Walking in the direction of the pool, he stopped under a willow several feet away from the water.

"No, señor," Taracahi said, pointing to the bath again.

Again, Acy obeyed.

Stepping out from the shade, he walked toward the fountain and came to a stop in a remnant of light left by the setting sun.

Taracahi opened his hand and offered it to Acy.

Acy looked at Taracahi's hand for a moment.

"I don't see anything there," he said, shaking his head.

"Sí, señor," Taracahi insisted, repeating the offer.

Again, Acy refused.

Taracahi smiled, pulled back his hand, and retrieved his gift.

Stepping beside the bird bath, he dipped his finger into the shallow pool, carefully carried a drop of water in his direction and suspended it over his palm.

Motioning for Acy to approach his hand, Taracahi again offered Acy his hand in gift.

"I told you. There's nothing there," he said, refusing.

Hunger twisted in Taracahi, but he smiled.

Lifting the water droplet and suspending it over his open palm, Taracahi raised it to his face and peered through the water. He motioned for Acy to do the same.

Acy obeyed.

Taking a step in Taracahi's direction, he stopped and bowed before Taracahi's hand.

Acy was in Taracahi's hand, peering through the water, when the sun moved in the water.

"Gold!" he exclaimed, an extra fleck in his eye. "That's gold! Where did you get it?"

"Sí, señor, " Taracahi answered calmly.

"In the desert? Where in the desert? Is there more? How much more? Big? How big?" Acy said, his face tingeing slightly as he held his cupped hands together.

Taracahi smiled.

"Big, big?" Acy asked again, his flush increasing.

Acy spread his hands apart, clutched an air boulder between them and swayed it back and forth.

"Big gold?" he asked, still swaying the stone.

Taracahi smiled again.

Then, in mid-sway, and without Taracahi having to fire an arrow, Acy changed colors.

Shifting calmly from red to white, he smiled and said calmly, "With that much gold a man could grow fat, feed his family for a year, you know,"

"Sí, señor."

"Come," Acy said, motioning for Taracahi to follow him away from the pool and back to the patio.

Day of Big Gold

Taracahi kept his eyes on Acy as he crossed the patio stones and followed him through the suspended ivy where his nest had been. In the mesa, the quail, sensing room for one more berry, twisted its neck sideways and pecked at one that lay craw close.

"Dinner's getting cold," Acy said standing in the doorway, "and as I said, cold beans don't belong in any man's stomach. Come on in."

Parting tendrils from the doorway, Acy passed through the strands and held the ivy high for Taracahi.

"It's one of man's gift from Nuestro Señor Our Lord to turn meat and milk into life, as my father used to say. Your father, Cajita, knew him. Life is more than work, he always used to say."

Inside, Acy led Taracahi to a spacious room adorned with wrought and encrusted heavy with furniture. Blankets Taracahi recognized from his childhood hung on the walls. Displayed among them was a portrait of Acy's father. In white pastels beside it hung a beautiful woman.

"My parents. Don Amado and Doña Purita," Acy said.

"Sí, señor."

"Here, you sit here," Acy said, pulling back one of two chairs. Two empty plates waited on the table.

"Jenny, honey," Acy called out to an adjacent room once he had seated Taracahi and was pulling a chair for himself, "we're going to need another plate."

A woman with the beauty of a doe stepping into sunlight from heavy timber appeared in the doorway. In her hand was the extra service Acy had requested.

"And this is my prize. My wife, Genoveva," he informed Taracahi, as he pulled out a chair and set it beside his own. Genoveva placed her dinnerware on the table and sat down. Realizing she had forgotten her fork, she rose and went back into the room.

"Jenny, how about an almaden?" Acy called after her. Then, addressing Taracahi, he said, "A meal without wine is a day without sparkle, mi amigo. That's what your father Cajita used to say. My father knew him well."

"Sí, señor."

Jenny returned with a tray on which were her fork, a slender bottle neatly corked, and three goblets. Acy reached for two, placed one before Taracahi, gave himself one, and left the other on the tray for Jenny. Reaching for the bottle, he pressed it to his chest. He worked the cork loose, and as the sweet mist gloved his hand, he addressed Taracahi.

"Quail or rabbit, mi amigo?" he asked, picking up Taracahi's plate. Placing it beside a platter where a beautiful quail was nestled in sprigs of mint and juniper, Acy drove his blade into the bird's heart, sliced off the tenders from both breasts, and placed them, boneless, in Taracahi's plate.

He placed the plate of prized flesh before Taracahi.

"Or both?" he said, already working the tip of his dagger along a loin of burnished hare. Having pried loose the long, choice length, Acy speared it with his own fork, lifted it over the dead quail, brushed it past the wine bottle, and laid it exquisitely beside the quail.

"Desert's full of 'em. Quail, too. Got me this one this afternoon," he said, returning his knife to the soulless lump on the platter. He severed off a slab of white and laid it across his plate.

"Good and fat. If you had come any other time of the year, mi amigo, we'd be looking at beans," he joked.

"Sí, señor."

"Soon's you're ready, there's some fruit," Acy continued.

He pointed with his fork.

"Apples."

He angled the knife's point toward the portraits on the wall.

"Good sweetness squeezed up from the earth," they both used to say. "That's this year's crop."

"Food's a beautiful thing, my father used to say," Acy continued, dividing what was left of the animals and reaching for Jenny's plate.

Turning away from the bones on Jenny's plate, Acy then addressed Taracahi.

"Let's not spoil this gift with words, amigo," he said. "I think we should eat first, then we will talk. ¿Que no?"

"Sí, señor."

Taracahi's plate was overflowing.

In the reflection of the goblet he was magnified, dark and cool as if under the bower of the desert willow. Cajita was right. Stealth was more a matter of waiting than walking.

Between slices of white, Acy glanced periodically in Taracahi's direction as the leather-lean Yaqui feasted in silence.

Acy smiled.

He would wait until Taracahi could hold no more food.

Taracahi pinched the final sliver of quail from his plate, drained his goblet, and with the sum dignity of Cajita and all the chieftains who had risen before him, placed it sentinel tall beside his empty plate.

"¿Poquito más? A little more?" Acy said, tipping the bottle toward Taracahi's empty glass.

"No, señor."

"Well, mi amigo," Acy continued, draining into his own goblet the dregs which Taracahi refused. "It's like my father used to say, and your father probably heard him many times. There's only one thing better than a full bottle, and that's the pleasure of seeing it empty."

Picking up his goblet, Acy swirled the refuse wine with its floating of skins and lifted it in Taracahi's direction.

"Salud."

"Sí, señor," acknowledged Taracahi, as he accepted the toast of victory.

"Salud," Acy greeted, in Jenny's direction. Then, still facing Jenny, he twisted his neck back toward Taracahi and said, "Now for some good plática, conversation, like my father used to say. This gold you have found..."

Master of the Tongue

"No, señor. No gold now," Taracahi said, a master now at the tongue he feared an hour ago. "I ask now for if big gold in some tomorrow. In day of wonder, I come to you with big gold. Cajita say your father tituli man, man of gold. Cahita wise. Say father and son one. Cajita, Taracahi. You, your father. Cajita know him. I know you."

Mrs. Tandemschnocker reads the last of Taracahi's words and looks up from the tablet. Amid the reflections in the thrift shop window she folds the cover back in place.

She looks at Big Chief and smiles.

She runs her hand lightly over his bonnet feathers.

She rises from the sill, taps the tablet lightly, and hands it back to me.

"Don't forget to sign it," she says, as she turns around and walks toward the canning shelf where she disappears into the glass rubble of the jars.

I sit alone in the bower of light with Big Chief.

His body, no longer flat and empty leaves, is springy soft and veined with ink.

I remember Altagracia on the hill. How she made a book from earth by clearing a patch of ground in a scattering of dry leaves. How she raked it with a dead stick. How she said, "...after you write it, you can write your name to it."

Lifting the lower corner of the tablet carefully so as not to disturb Big Chief's feathers, I insert the pen sideways and claim my name.

Mío.

Books by Farolito Press

Poetry:
Musings of a Barrio Sack Boy by L. Luis López
A Painting of Sand by L. Luis López

Fiction:
No Lack of Lonesome by Albino Gonzales
A Destiny is Sworn by Rhianwen Roberts (forthcoming)

Farolito Press
P.O. Box 60003
Grand Junction, CO 81506
(970) 243-5940 e-mail: melop2@aol.com